PEREGRINATION

A Novel

WALTENEGUS DARGIE

LAMSI PUBLISHING

PEREGRINATION

Also by **WALTENEGUS DARGIE**

The Eunuch and the King's Daughter

The Reason for Life

ERMIAS

To

Josh

Prologue

The old man spent much of the evening preoccupied and a little vexed with himself. Having already made up his mind to make one final journey to the Great Mountain alone, he could not bring himself to tell the boy his decision. Tomorrow they would travel to a remote village where they would be very busy for three successive days. There they would have no time to themselves to talk about anything privately.

The boy was lying on his back beside him, fixing his gaze on the full moon hovering above. Either guessing what was bothering the old man or anticipating the demands of the coming days or simply not being in the mood to talk, he had been unusually quiet. Both were physically exhausted. They had covered more than twenty-five kilometers on foot that day. Still, they were patiently waiting for the last twigs to burn completely before they retired to their tent.

"He will insist on coming with me," the old man thought for the tenth time. "He thinks he's old enough to understand everything, but he's mistaken. I can't delay this decision any longer, though. I must tell him."

It was a quiet, cloudless evening. He studied the boy's profile with studious curiosity and then calmly shifted his attention to the village below. But the village was too far away to be distinguished in the moonlight. Finally, he rested his gaze on the misty mountain in front of them which stood so tall that it resembled the shadow of a giant. "If I raise the subject now," he thought, "it'll make for a long and involved discussion and there'll be very little sleep. Then he'll be too tired for the journey tomorrow. I should have told him, should have prepared him a long time ago. It's better to tell him tomorrow on our way to the village. I've enough time to explain to him and he has enough time to process my decision."

For a brief moment he thought of sending him on an errand to one of the nearby villages on the eve of his departure, but he felt uneasy about it. That would be unkind and it would break the boy's heart when he found out. Another option was to get up very early in the morning and leave him a note, explaining everything.

"No, it's better to explain in person," he reasoned silently, without shifting his gaze from the mountain. "Even though it's not an easy task, it has to be done. Why should I worry so much?" he asked himself, for once shifting his attention to himself. "Don't I know he'll be all right? He'll be fine. He'll triumph."

He stood up.

"Well, son," he said languidly. "The fire is going out. We have to sleep now. A long journey awaits us in the morning."

The boy stood up lethargically and poured water on the smoldering fire. The old man went inside and the boy followed him. They said good night and the boy fell asleep immediately, but the old man spent much of the night praying. After his prayers, he felt peaceful, and, determined to announce his decision tomorrow, fell into a heavy sleep. Very early in the morning he heard the boy calling him.

"I'm awake, just give me some time," the old man mumbled without much thought, meaning to get up.

But he fell back to sleep. Then he heard the boy calling him for the second time.

"Get up and set your things in order. It's time to set off."

"I will, my son. Just give me a minute to say a prayer."

But for the second time the old man fell back to sleep. After some time, he heard the boy calling him for the third time.

"I'm sorry, I fell back to sleep twice. We must set off, I know," he muttered apologetically and stood up with some difficulty.

The day was breaking but inside it was still dark.

"Will you dismantle the tent while I go and wash?" he asked the boy, searching for his sandals in the dark.

But the boy did not answer him.

"Where are you, my son?" the old man inquired, now searching for the boy with his eyes.

He could not see him. He went outside and looked around, but the boy was not around. A huge sun was rising behind the tent and the sky was cloudless.

"Where could he be?" the old man wondered aloud and went inside.

"Samuel," he called louder.

There was no reply.

"Samuel!" he called still louder.

But there was no answer. He went outside once again and searched for the boy. Then he saw him coming towards the tent, carrying a water can on his shoulder.

"Oh, you went to fetch water!" he said with a relief.

"I wanted you to sleep a little longer, so I went to fetch water."

"Didn't you try to wake me up?"

"No, I didn't."

"But I heard you calling me three times."

"No, I didn't. I went out cautiously in order not to disturb you. You stayed up very late last night."

The old man looked confused.

"Yes, yes, I did," he muttered. "How did you know? I thought you'd fallen asleep."

The boy stood in front of the old man and rested the water can on the ground.

"It's all right if you travel to the Great Mountain alone. I've come to terms with it."

The old man was taken aback, so that he did not react immediately.

"The thought has been weighing on you the past few weeks," the boy added, fixing his eyes on the ground.

"I've organized everything, so that you don't have any problems while I'm away."

"I'll be gone when you're away."

"Where will you be going?"

"I have a task to accomplish."

"Are you going to your parents?"

The boy regarded the old man silently.

"Where else do you want to go?"

The boy remained silent.

"I see," the old man reacted after some time.

"You must trust me."

"Of course," the old man replied, the expression on his face conveying great concern. "Are you going far?"

"I don't know yet."

"I knew I must let you go one day," the old man murmured. Both were silent for a while.

"Don't worry about me, I'll be fine. Our lives are in the hands of God," the boy broke the silence, going to dismantle the tent.

"I know, my son, I know," the old man muttered, tears blurring his vision.

Chapter 1

Standing on top of a modest hill, Danny watched an enemy jet dashing towards the facility which had recently been erected to treat wounded soldiers. For a fraction of a second his reaction was that of fascination, but it very quickly dissipated into disbelief and shock. Instinctively, he covered his ears tightly with his hands. The jet swiftly descended and discharged its ominous contents. Then, releasing an ear-splitting noise, it ascended into the sky and vanished from sight. Another deafening and reverberating noise followed when the bombs detonated on the facility. Within the blink of an eye the facility erupted in a cloud of dense black smoke, from which an unfurling ball of fire emerged. The boy's legs shook violently and gave way. He collapsed onto the ground.

He could not tell how long he had lain unconscious, but he regained consciousness of his own accord. He tried to get up, meaning to rush to the facility, to search for his father and adoptive sister, but his body refused to comply. He attempted to turn his head, but it felt like a heavy metal ball. He closed his eyes and tried to breathe deeply. His back was hurting. Moreover, the entirety of his surroundings smelt of an offensive mixture of burning medicine and dead bodies. He opened his eyes with determination and once again tried to turn his face towards the facility. With great difficulty he managed this time.

Where the facility had once stood there was now a heap of burning wood and aluminum sheets along with the dismembered parts of dead bodies. Nearby there was a commotion of soldiers and of vehicles. A little farther away, he saw four or five pickup trucks rushing in different directions.

"It's over," the boy mumbled with a broken heart.

He meant for his father and sister. He had left the two of them the previous evening in that same facility. It was clear to him that there was nothing left for him to return to. As he cried silently, he felt his tears trickling into his right ear.

"Are you all right?" he suddenly heard a voice calling.

Before he was able to turn his face, he saw a handsome boy standing in front of him.

"Are you all right?" the newcomer repeated his question, kneeling down quickly in front of Danny and closely examining his face with his small and alert brown eyes.

He had a small handsome face, cheerful and fresh, not at all the sort of burnt, dusty, sweaty faces one often saw in the small town. His nose and lips were also small, but proportional and delightful to look at. He wore a wide-brimmed straw hat beneath which one could see his long and curly hair.

For a second, Danny thought he was dreaming or hallucinating, on account of his fall and the morning heat, but the boy stretched out his hand, meaning to support him to rise to his feet. Danny took the hand and made an effort, but he released a sharp groan and swiftly released the hand.

"Hurry up, we must leave this place at once. The war will break out any moment now."

The boy stretched out his hand once again. This time Danny took hold of it and managed to sit up.

"You must get up at once. You're fine. You're only shocked, that's all. You saw the jet coming, didn't you?"

Danny nodded feebly, still sitting.

"Come on, get up. We should hurry."

With the support of the stranger, Danny got up on his feet. "How are you?" the boy inquired looking worried and examining Danny with his alert eyes.

"It hurts everywhere. I must have bumped my head on the ground. My back and ribs are also hurting."

"If we don't leave this place at once, we'll be caught by invading troops. This is the only high place in this area. Both enemy and friendly soldiers will be keen to occupy it as quickly as possible. It's a wonder that it hasn't been occupied already."

"Our soldiers have been posted to guard this hill, I'm sure of it. There should also be two anti-aircraft autocannons deployed somewhere."

His father had disclosed this piece of information to him last night at supper.

"I wonder how they were unable to bring down the accursed jet?"

"They must have been hiding in their stronghold when they saw the jet surging past. Hurry up, please! We must leave this place at once. We should find our way to Neghelle."

"Neghelle?" Danny retorted.

"Where else can we go?"

"But Neghelle is very far from here, how can we get there?"

"We shall find out along the way, but now we must leave this place and bring ourselves to safety. Come on, hurry up."

"Shouldn't we rather go back to the camp?"

"With all this commotion going on? Besides, civilians were told to evacuate the camp weeks ago."

Danny considered their situation to be hopeless, but he realized that he could not return to the camp. Neither could he stay any longer on the hill. Neghelle was more than three hundred kilometers away and between here and there lay a vast wilderness, not to mention the hazards of the scorching sun and the unknown nomads dwelling in the wilderness. What did this boy mean by "finding" their way to Neghelle? Surely not crossing the wilderness on foot?

"Who are you? I haven't seen you before in the camp." Danny asked the boy.

"I'm not from here. I came here by chance. I'll explain later. Now hurry up."

Danny obeyed reluctantly. Yet he found the boy's voice pleasant and encouraging and he was glad that he was not alone. The boys turned their backs on the camp and hurriedly descended the hill on the other side. There was no one in the vicinity.

The boy was a little older than Danny, but not by more than one or two years. He looked healthier, sturdier, and more agile than Danny, and, for his age, he was fearless. He was wearing khaki shorts and a disproportionately large summer jacket matching the color of his shorts. His sandals were made of goatskin, the sort of sandals worn by the children of the surrounding nomads. In his right hand he was holding a decorated staff which was approximately as long as he was tall. Over his left shoulder he was carrying an old and dirty leather shoulder bag. Had it not been for the seriousness of the situation, he would have looked like a comic figure.

They hurried down the hill, the stranger in front, leading by a couple of meters, and Danny trying his best to keep up. It was still early in the morning, but the sun had already started to scorch everything in sight. There was no sign of trees or bushes as far as the eye could see, only red dust and numerous anthills.

When they finished descending the hill, the boy removed a round army water bottle from his bag and offered it to Danny.

"Here," he said, "drink, but don't drink too much at once."

Danny was thirsty but controlled himself and drank just enough.

"Here," the boy removed two military biscuits from his bag and offered them to Danny.

"Where did you get them?" Danny asked him after taking the biscuits thankfully.

"I met a group of soldiers yesterday evening just outside the camp and they gave them to me."

"Just so?"

"Why, there are kind people everywhere!"

"Are you trying to bribe me?"

"Why should I bribe you? If you refuse to go with me, it's your right. Feel free to go back to the camp. I'll march on all alone. I'm accustomed to travelling alone."

"Who are you?"

"I spent several days in this terrain searching for someone, but I was not successful. Finally, I decided to search for him elsewhere."

"Your father?"

"No, but he's like a father to me."

"If you met a group of soldiers yesterday, why didn't you ask them to send you back to Neghelle in one of the military trucks? Trucks depart for Neghelle almost every day."

He himself had come to Dolo from Neghelle four days ago hidden inside a cargo truck.

"That's because I don't want to go to Neghelle directly. I'll have to search for my old man in multiple places."

"Where are you from?"

"Oh, what's it to you, where I come from?"

"But a while ago you said we should go to Neghelle."

"That's because I know you want to go to Neghelle."

"How do you know?"

"Why, are you not from Neghelle? Almost all the soldiers in the camp have families in Neghelle."

"Why should I come with you if you're not going to Neghelle?"

"You've no other option. I'll help you get to Neghelle. I know my way around."

"How can I trust a complete stranger? I don't know who you are, I don't know where you're going, and I don't know what you're up to."

"As you please. I'm going."

The boy gently lifted up his hat as a sign of saying goodbye, turned his back on Danny, and moved on.

"I'll go to the main road and wait for a truck heading to Neghelle. I'll beg the driver to take me with him," Danny shouted, his own voice sounding unconvincing to him.

The boy stopped briefly and turned his face towards Danny. "It's very unlikely any trucks will leave for Neghelle today. You'd better trust me. Trucks may arrive from Neghelle, loaded with soldiers and ammunitions and other supplies, but they'll not risk taking us with them into the camp. Besides, we'll be a great burden and nuisance to them. As you may already know, the inhabitants of the town were ordered to leave the place a long time ago."

"The soldiers know me. If they see me, they'll help me."

"I doubt that. How did you manage to enter into the camp in the first place? Children are not allowed to enter the camp."

"I came to visit my father four days ago. He's a doctor."

"But children are not allowed to enter the camp, why did they let you in?"

"As you can see, I was allowed to go in."

"You sneaked into the camp unnoticed, didn't you?"

"That's none of your business."

"Granted you were permitted to go in, how did you manage to get out of the camp? The camp is tightly guarded. You yourself have said so."

"Never mind how I managed to get out."

Looking at his pleasant face and listening to his cheerful voice, Danny found it difficult to imagine that the boy could do him any harm.

"I'll not harm you," the boy shouted presently, as if reading his mind.

"Which way should we take then?"

"We should head to the river and follow it. It'll lead us to Neghelle and will supply us with water and fish."

"But the river follows a zigzag route; I've seen it on the map. It'll be a very long journey."

"You're correct, but that's the only option we have. At any rate, we should follow the river for at least part of the way. If we take the main road, we shall soon be scorched by the sun and die of thirst and too much sweating."

"But the nomads will certainly find and may even kill us if we follow the river."

"You may be right, but we shall be careful. The river is our only hope."

Presently, the boys saw a military helicopter taking off and heading in the direction of Neghelle, most likely transporting wounded soldiers from the jet attack earlier.

"One of them could be my father," Danny thought anxiously.

"Hurry up," he heard the boy urging him.

Danny joined the boy and they hurried towards the River Ganale. From the hill the river appeared to be not too far away but it took them more than thirty minutes to get there. By the time they arrived, the sun was already hot and they both were sweating and tired. Danny collapsed on the dry ground next to the river.

"We should make every effort to put as many kilometers behind us as possible," said the boy, sitting beside Danny. "It's very likely that the enemy will swarm this area in the coming days. I'm not sure if our soldiers are well prepared for the war. The only hope is that the initial enemy attack is by air, since they cannot cross the border with vehicles and artillery without first crossing the bridges. This'll give us some time."

"But the enemy don't need a bridge to cross into the country, do they? Besides, how can it give us hope if they attack by air first?"

"The antiaircraft missiles will not allow enemy jets to penetrate deep into our territory, which is why. As to the bridges, the enemy need them to safely transport their tanks and other vehicles."

Danny was not encouraged by this statement. He felt rather miserable and hopeless. Besides, he was now struggling to suppress the cough that was pushing up with full force, on the brink of eruption. He lay flat on the ground on his belly and coughed continuously for a long time.

"You look very ill," the boy observed meanwhile, kneeling beside Danny and handing him the water bottle to drink.

The cough subsided at long last and Danny sat down on the ground and tried to drink from the water bottle. But the cough returned and he held his nose tightly. He coughed for a long time once again. Afterwards, having completely exhausted himself of all energy, he lay down on the ground and closed his eyes and slept instantly.

Chapter 2

When he woke up, he noticed that the boy had put his jacket on his head to protect him from the sun. The boy himself was sitting beside him, grilling fish.

"I've caught two fish, but it took me a long time. The fish here are crafty," the boy observed, somehow sensing that Danny was awake.

"Where did you get the gear to fish with and to make fire?"

"I had them all with me inside my bag. Get up and eat," he said cheerfully.

"What's the time?"

"I've no idea. But it looks like we may not be able to advance that much today. We'll have to make the attempt, nevertheless."

When he removed the jacket from his head, he saw that the sun was tilting towards the western horizon. He must have slept for a long time.

"Did I cough in my sleep?"

"Yes, many times, terribly. Here, take this."

The boy offered Danny one of the grilled fish, twice as big as the palm of his hand and full of meat. Danny sat up and ate greedily. The boy ate the other fish. When they were finished, the boy got up and extinguished the fire by spreading red soil over it to make sure that the fire pit was indistinguishable.

"We must try not to leave visible traces behind us. You never know who may get the fancy to follow us. Can you get up?"

He helped Danny get up and they walked along the river, opposite to its course of flow, northwards.

"Are you sure this is the right thing to do?" Danny asked the boy anxiously.

"I suppose I'm right," was his reply.

"What's your name?"

"My name is Samuel and yours?"

"Mine is Daniel but everybody calls me Danny."

"A great name. I hope you'll survive a month or so in the wilderness."

"Do you think it'll take us that long to get to Neghelle?"

"Oh, yes, or perhaps a bit longer than that."

"How do you know?"

"It took me about three Sundays to get here. Since you look ill and feeble, it'll take us more than that."

Danny wanted to protest that he was not feeble, but abandoned the idea. His frailty and sickness were evident. "You haven't told me about yourself," he complained instead, after they walked in silence for a while.

"There isn't much to know about me," Samuel answered dismissively. "I was someone's assistant for a long time. Then I parted company with my old man because I had some business to take care of and he had a journey to make. But I missed my old man. When, after some time, I returned to the appointed place, he wasn't there. Since then I've been wandering in the wilderness searching for him, but I haven't found him yet."

"What do you mean by you haven't found him, he just disappeared?"

"He's never settled in any one place for long."

"How long were you separated before you went in search of him?"

"I suppose long enough."

"How long have you been searching for him?"

"For a long time. I'm not good at numbers, by the way. Never went to school, even though I can read and write very well."

"What's your relationship to the old man?"

"He's been like a father to me. He brought me up."

"You have no parents?"

"I have. But they didn't raise me."

"Why?"

"Because my mother made a vow when I was a child."

"What kind of a vow?"

"She was childless, so she went to a prophet, who became like a father to me, and asked him to pray for her. Before anyone asked her, she made this promise that if God heard the prophet's prayer and gave her a child, she would dedicate the child to God and he would serve the prophet all his life. Apparently, the prayer of the prophet was answered and she kept her promise."

"You mean you grew up without your mother?"

"She raised me until I was big enough to be given up. I can't tell how old I was when I was given to the prophet, perhaps three or four, I don't know. But I was a small boy when she brought me to the prophet."

"Then she never saw you again?"

"In the beginning she visited me whenever she could, but as time went by, she saw me only occasionally because the prophet moved around from place to place so frequently."

"Do you mean, your mother gave you up to a complete stranger and forgot about you? How about your father?"

"You don't understand. The prophet was not a complete stranger."

Danny could not believe a word Samuel said. He was aware of these so-called prophets, wise men, fortune-tellers, and all. They had populated every high hill around Neghelle and beyond. His mother had taken him to so many of them, so that they could pray for his health or tell her his fortune or make supplication on his behalf to God or other gods. For he had been very sickly from childhood. None of them had helped. Indeed, his health had grown worse and his mother had wasted a large amount of money.

Samuel seemed to have accurately read Danny's mind, for he turned to him with a weak smile and looked at him keenly.

"You don't believe a word I've said, do you?"

"My mother has been deceived by many of the so-called prophets or men-of-God," Danny confessed dejectedly.

"The prophet was different, though. But I don't ask you to believe me. Tell me about yourself, why and how did you come to Dolo?"

"I came to visit my father. He's a surgeon."

"But you should still be in school, how could your mother allow you to travel to one of the most dangerous places in the country on your own?"

"I didn't tell my mother where I was going. She doesn't know where I am."

"There you have told the truth. For you decided to abscond without her knowledge and hid yourself inside a military cargo truck to come to Dolo."

"You have guessed correctly."

"The question is: why did you do that?"

"Can we change the subject?"

Danny was irritated by Samuel's pointed questions. In addition, he was experiencing side stitches and his cough was threatening to erupt with full force once again. They walked in silence, but before long he began coughing so hard that he had to stop walking.

"This isn't working, please go ahead without me. I can't make it," he told Samuel in tears as soon as he was able to catch his breath.

In truth, he was desperately wishing Samuel to stay with him, for he was apprehensive lest Samuel change his mind and carry on without him when he realized how ill he was. He was accustomed to being rejected. Many children at his school had rejected him when they realized how ill he was. He had been persuaded that his father had left them because he was dying.

"I'm not a coward. I'll not leave you alone in your condition," Samuel said presently and handed Danny his water bottle.

Danny wanted to vehemently protest, not because he had a reason to, but simply because he thought that it was how a boy in his condition should react when he was shown great kindness. But Samuel's kind face and gentle smile disarmed him and put him at ease.

"Believe me, it's only the beginning which seems insurmountable," Samuel reassured him.

After a short break, they continued on their journey. This time they walked for more than two hours, much of the time in silence. In the meantime, however, Samuel waded into the river multiple times to refill his bottle and to pour the water over his head. He invited Danny to do the same, but Danny was worried about his lungs, so he declined the offer even though the heat was unbearable to him and he was sweating profusely. But occasionally he went to the river and covered his feet in wet sand to cool them down. Towards sundown Samuel stopped.

"We should now take a proper rest here. We both are exhausted and you look very ill. The best thing about our journey so far is that we have left the town and the camp behind us for good, however long the distance between here and our destination may appear. Which means we're determined to carry on with our journey. Once a decision is made, carrying out the plan is not so difficult."

They were standing on an elevated place from which they could see the silently flowing river shimmering in the sunlight like a silvery snake. There were bushes of modest height and density on both sides of the river. Without waiting for Danny's consent, Samuel descended the elevation and spent some time searching for a suitable place to rest. At last he found a dry place covered with clean pebbled sand and surrounded by a handful of bushes.

"We shall rest here for now but in the night, we should sleep in the open," he said, beckoning Danny to descend.

He drew a wide circle with his staff in the dirt of the open space next to their intended place of rest in order to designate the location for the campfire.

"We need to collect twigs to make a fire. I can tell you from experience that the nights in the wilderness are biting unless we have a fire."

"But where can we find twigs?"

"We shall find enough to burn the whole night."
Danny sat on the pebbled sand, in the shade of the bushes, and asked Samuel to hand him the water bottle. Samuel gave him the water bottle, removed his hat, the bag, the jacket, and his shoes.

"I'll share with you some of the things I've learnt while travelling with the prophet," he said, leaning on his staff. "Maybe you already know them, but I shall tell you anyway. In order to survive in the wilderness, we should rest a lot during the day and travel as much as we can between sunset and sunrise. Besides avoiding the danger of travelling in the open and in the scorching heat, the time before sunrise is the coolest in the wilderness. Therefore, it's better to walk than to sleep during this time. Secondly, hyenas and other wild animals are less likely to attack us if we are moving. Speaking of hyenas, you should know that our greatest foes in this journey are hyenas, particularly, the spotted ones. I've seen a handful of them with my own eyes, but the soldiers I've talked to yesterday also warned me against them. Of course, we should also be careful of lions, jackals, and all, but the chances of meeting them here in the wilderness are small. In any case, whenever we camp, we have to protect ourselves from wild animals, including snakes. We should always sleep in the open and leave a fire burning. One of us should stay awake, besides."

Samuel spoke matter-of-factly like an experienced soldier and gave Danny further instructions as to how they should protect themselves. When he was finished, he told Danny to rest, but he himself left to collect twigs. Danny was too exhausted to offer him any help. He consented to Samuel's suggestion and lay down on the bare ground on his side and closed his eyes to sleep.

But, as much as he wished to sleep, he was not able to do so. Instead, he fixed his eyes vacantly at the clean pebbles and tried to think about what awaited them ahead and his own fate in it. It was very likely that he would die in the wilderness in the coming days. He had been wasting away for a long time, even though his family and all the rest had tried to conceal the truth from him. That is, until yesterday evening, when he accidentally overheard his father making the dreadful admission to his adoptive sister, Zema...

Chapter 3

Zema had been away in Neghelle for six days, accompanying the delegate who was responsible for transporting medical supplies and facilities to the base in Dolo. On the day of her return, the three of them had supper together and after supper she made coffee and they talked about the latest developments. Thereafter his father retired to his room, saying he had to get up early in the morning to supervise some of the soldiers he had operated on that day. As soon as the father had left, Zema turned to Danny angrily.

"You haven't acted responsibly; you rascal! Faé is dying of anxiety and the poor woman has no idea you are here. How dare you disappear like that, without telling anyone where you were going?"

"I don't care," he mumbled defiantly, avoiding her eyes.

"You've never cared. You're a little selfish devil. How much she's suffered, the poor woman, on account of you!"

"She'll have her peace soon."

"You're shameless! That's what you are."

Zema cleared the table and swept the floor. Then, mumbling good night, she left. Danny remained in his seat, dejectedly staring at the table and struggling to contain the rage and tears which were fighting for vehement manifestation. With great patience he controlled himself, knowing very well what would ensue if he lost self-control. Then he stood up, switched off the light and went to bed.

He had unusually been well the entire evening. Hoping to fall asleep immediately, he closed his eyes, but he could not sleep. His mind was alert and full of thoughts and regrets. He felt very sorry for not having let his mother know where he had gone and for lying to his father. He was very sorry for his mother, for her lonely struggle and suffering. He was very sorry for his two little brothers and his little sister and felt terribly guilty for having been the cause of perpetual sober mood in the family.

Long after his father and Zema had left, Danny continued to stare into the darkness and thought about death and what lay in wait after that. Then he heard the door noiselessly opened and seen the silhouette of Zema coming in and going towards his father's chamber without making a sound. Suddenly he become alert, a distressing suspicion he never knew existed coming to life.

"What does this all mean? Is she sleeping with him?" the question burst forth in his mind.

His mother had been accusing his father of unfaithfulness for a long time. Yet the very notion of his father sleeping with Zema seemed absurd to him.

An irresistible desire to go and see what they were up to gripped him, but he was very much afraid lest his cough betray his presence. Lying alert and still staring into the darkness, he felt his heart racing wildly. He nearly persuaded himself to give up his quest but the impulse to get up and witness what they were up to seemed to stifle him to death. After a fierce struggle, he finally got out of his bed cautiously and tiptoed in the dark towards his father's chamber. The front curtain was drawn and the light inside was switched off, but Danny could hear their measured voices.

"How long?" he heard Zema asking calmly.

"Perhaps six months, perhaps even less. But not more than a year," his father, too, answered calmly.

Something told Danny that they were talking about him.

"The poor boy!"

"He won't miss anything if he dies. My only wish is that it happens swiftly."

"The poor boy. His life has been full of troubles and suffering."

His father released a long sigh. Danny felt as if he had heard his executioner's final utterance.

"Now let's leave the boy alone and mind our own business."

"You have missed me, haven't you?"

"Six endless days."

Danny could not stay there a moment longer. His heart became very heavy within him and he wanted to sit down. Dragging himself to his bed with the same caution he had exercised in coming, he sat down on the military bed. The news of his own inevitable death stunned him. After a moment of numbness and immobility, his whole body began to tremble violently and he fell on the narrow bed, supine. In that instant he was certain that the end was coming and he was glad about it. Much to his regret, nonetheless, the spasm left him and gradually he slipped into an uneasy sleep.

He woke up before any of them and instantly decided to leave that place, even though he had no idea where he could go. It was still dark inside but he found his way to the wardrobe where his father hung his military clothes. He removed one of the military jackets and went out. Outside was complete darkness and a cold wind was blowing. Despite tight security presence inside the camp, he managed to walk quickly towards the fence and blindly found a spot where he could crawl under the fence. The fence was made of barbed-wire, but was poorly constructed.

"Oh, God!" he whispered to himself once outside, "Why was I created? Why was I born? I can't take it anymore! I can't stand it any longer."

He wept bitterly until he had no strength left…

Chapter 4

Samuel returned towards sundown carrying a load of twigs on his shoulder.

"Now get up and help me prepare the fire," he told Danny putting down the twigs.

Danny got up and prepared the twigs for a campfire. Meanwhile, Samuel chose some of the twigs and began sharpening them with a small knife. He seemed skillful with the knife.

"What are they for?" Danny asked him.

"If a wild animal attacks us, these will be useful for fighting back."

"How can we fight a wild animal with them?"

"First, we shall simply try to frighten it. But if it decides to be impertinent, then we should use these as knives. Most of the wild animals in the wilderness are not big. We should use our heads when we fight and aim to attack where it hurts. His eyes, for instance, or his ears, his nose, his stomach. Never aim at its head or at any other part of the body which is hard. Neither should you fight aimlessly."

"I've never fought a wild animal before."

"Neither have I. But now that there's a good chance of coming face to face with a wild animal, we must prepare ourselves for any eventuality."

"You seem to be very skillful and thoroughly prepared for this journey."

"You have paid me a great compliment."

Darkness descended quickly, but Samuel was in no hurry to light the fire. He removed his oversized jacket, spread it on the ground, and lay down on it on his back. Feeling still exhausted, Danny likewise lay down on the ground still wearing his father's jacket.

"We should dispense with eating the biscuits tonight. We should keep them as long as we can and feed only on fish whenever we can, because the supply of fish is never certain."

Danny did not object.

"You weren't planning to return to the camp this morning when I met you on the hill," Samuel observed in the meantime.

"How did you know?"

"I could tell from your look."

"I had a fight with my father last night," Danny lied.

"You seem to be very ill and very upset."

Danny's first impulse was to contradict Samuel, to deny that he was very ill, but he did not have energy for contradiction.

"It's not your fault, you know."

Danny felt a familiar explosive anger rising up within him, but after a struggle, managed to contain it. He had no energy even for anger. They lay down in silence for a long time, Danny gazing at the stars with unyielding fascination.

"The firmament is awesome to behold at night in the wilderness. I love the wilderness at night," Samuel observed presently.

It was still hot and the hot air was suffocating, but in the sky countless stars were emerging as if being generously sown by an invisible hand. Danny was filled with a deep and inexplicable yearning for something which he could not put his finger on, a desperate longing for something beyond his reach. His eyes filled with hot tears. Was he jealous of the stars, jealous of the peace, the aloofness, and the brilliance they were enjoying, none of which he was sharing? By contrast, his life was devoid of peace; he felt insignificant, undesirable, and useless; he was incapable of existing without the support and care of others.

Then he heard the gentle snoring of Samuel.

"How unfortunate!" he thought.

He was dreading staying awake all by himself and was also a little jealous of Samuel's apparent healthy and confident existence. But he quickly checked himself, remembering how Samuel had been selfless and caring, toiling alone much of the time for their safety and wellbeing.

Gradually, he, too, slumbered. But he could not sleep long. He woke up, feeling all at once very hot and very cold, his back and his face covered with sweat and his cough erupting with full force. He coughed very hard for a long time. In his despair he silently begged God for this battle to end. In a matter of seconds, he relinquished the struggle and passed out.

When he regained consciousness, the fire was burning and Samuel was sitting on the bare ground next to the fire and Danny was lying down on his father's jacket, covered with Samuel's jacket.

"It seems to be a peaceful night. We're lucky," Samuel spoke without turning his face towards Danny.

"I'm sorry, I fell asleep," Danny apologized, nursing a guilty conscience.

"It's all right," Samuel replied simply.

Despite the severe attack he had endured, he now felt a lightness in his chest and could breathe with relative ease. He wanted to join Samuel by the fire but felt boneless and very feeble. So, he stayed in his place and gazed at the stars, which had multiplied in quantity and become brighter and nearer.

"Will there be peace after death?" he asked himself, his eyes moist with warm tears and feeling utterly helpless.

It was impossible not to envy the stars.

"My father was killed this morning," he told Samuel without actually intending to.

"I suspected," Samuel replied calmly.

"How?"

"I read it in your eyes this morning. He was hit by the bombs the jet dropped, correct?"

Danny could not answer him. He was overcome with sorrow and dissolved into tears. But his weeping quickly gave way to another round of hard and dry coughing. Samuel rushed to his aid. Kneeling down in front of Danny, he gently pressed one of his hands on his chest and the other on his forehead.

"Let go of your sorrow, let it go. For otherwise it'll kill you," Samuel exhorted Danny gently.
Danny felt the warmth of Samuel's hands.
This time the cough relented. Then Samuel carefully put Danny down on his side, tucked his own jacket around him, and sat beside him. Soon Danny fell asleep once again.

Chapter 5

Danny awoke with an urgent sensation that Samuel had gone on his journey without him. It was still dark and the fire was smoldering. He got up in a panic and called Samuel quietly. There was no answer. He looked carefully around and kept on calling Samuel, now a little louder, but there was no response. As he searched carefully, he realized that Samuel's bag was gone, but not his jacket. He returned to his place, put on his father's jacket, and sat on the ground next to the fire, not knowing what to do next. Then he saw a shadow approaching from the southern side of the river towards the fire. It was Samuel's silhouette.

"You frightened me," Danny whispered reproachfully.

"I heard your voice but had to sit still in order not to frighten the fish away."

Samuel had caught a handful of small fish which he carefully placed on the pebbled sand by the fire.

"The best time to fish is before sunrise," he said with a satisfied voice as he placed some twigs on the smoldering fire.

"I thought you had gone on without me."

"Why would I do that?"

"I don't know, maybe I'm a burden and a hindrance to you?"

"Nonsense."

"Did the twigs last the whole night?"

"I saved some in order to grill the fish."

"Why did you take your bag with you?"

"We mustn't leave food near us when we sleep. The smell of food attracts wild animals and they will end up attacking us."

He knelt down and, supporting himself with his right hand and leaning forward, blew into the fire. The fire crackled back to life and Samuel began grilling the fish.

"Do you travel a lot with your prophet?" Danny asked him.

"Sure," he answered.

"Where?"

"To different places. The prophet rarely stays in one place. He loves travelling from place to place, visiting people who need his help. Most of them are ill or distraught people looking for comfort and encouragement. He has the gift of knowing which of the people need him most."

"Is he revered and feared?"

"What a question you ask!"

"Is he rich?"

"Certainly not."

"The wise men and fortune-tellers to whom my mother took me were very rich and greatly revered."

"My prophet never accepts money for his service, in any form."

"How does he exist then?"

"He does exist somehow. If we stayed in one place long enough, we would keep our own garden where we would plant vegetables and the likes. Admittedly, he sometimes accepts gifts from people who can afford it, but never in return for a favor and never from rich people."

"Why doesn't he take money from rich people?"

"I'm not sure if he has a specific reason."

"What's he like?"

"He's an ordinary old man, you know. Probably you wouldn't notice him if you chanced upon him."

"Does he keep long and unkempt hair, a beard or moustache, does he wear dirty overcoat?"

Samuel laughed heartily.

"He isn't someone you can describe by his external appearance."

"Does he heal the sick?"

"Healing isn't his gift. Though, yes, occasionally he even heals the sick, mostly children. But I can't tell how. Every time it's done differently. It's not an art one can master, you know, being a prophet. It's a gift you can't take for granted."

"What's the gift of your prophet?"

"Bringing messages. Which's why he is called a prophet."

"What kind of messages?"

"All sorts."

"From whom?"

"It's difficult to explain to ordinary people. I don't mean to insult you. But the people who receive the messages understand from whom they've received them. A person who doesn't expect a message doesn't understand it if he's given one."

"How long before the morning breaks?" Danny asked, wishing to change the subject.

"Not long. We shall set out as soon as I've finished grilling the fish and we've eaten our breakfast. Unfortunately, we may not be able to cover a great distance today on account of your illness, but we shall travel as much as we can and as long as the sun allows."

Danny was hungry and his lips and throat were dry. His heart was aching with yearning for something to which he could not assign a name. What sorts of messages did the prophet bring to the people? Were they real and were they really helpful, the messages? Had he really healed the children? How did he do it? Who was this prophet?

He desperately wished Samuel's account to be true, to contain a grain of truth, one-hundredth of the truth. Had the prophet really been sent by someone? It was the existence of this someone which gave Danny a heartache, not the messages, not the healings, as such.

Chapter 6

Just before sunrise the boys were frightened by the sudden and piercing sound of two jets flying overhead towards Dolo. About four or five minutes later they watched the southern horizon being set ablaze.

"It seems that our troops are finally returning the favor," observed Danny with apparent satisfaction.

"We must get up at once and press on," said Samuel, gathering his belongings.

They were nearly finished with breakfast, so they quickly extinguished the fire and carefully covered the pit with sand. Samuel wrapped the rest of the fish with leaves he had cut from a nearby shrub and put it inside his bag. And they left the place in a hurry.

Throughout the journey Danny was apprehensive lest his cough reassert itself, forcing them to interrupt their travel. Indeed, they had hardly walked for half an hour when he started to cough. At first, at longer intervals, but, as they progressed, the cough increased both in magnitude and in frequency, so that he had to stop walking altogether. For the first time in more than two months, he also began to spit blood. He knew that he was paying the price for refusing to take his medicine.

"I'd rather spit blood all day long and die as a consequence than take that repugnant medicine," he muttered forcefully, as if defending himself from an invisible accuser.

His entire being had detested the medicine. Even the memory of it was insufferable. Samuel wisely kept quiet and sat beside Danny. One word from him and Danny would have exploded with rage and collapsed on the spot. Fortunately, despite the terrible cough, he managed to keep down the food he had just eaten and the cough subsided at long last. Samuel silently offered him the water bottle but Danny had no strength left to take a sip. He threw himself on the ground and closed his eyes, feeling miserable and guilty.

The sun was rising over the grey eastern horizon like a huge red ball of fire. There was no mountain or hill above or from behind which it had emerged. It emerged, as it were, out of nowhere and floated in space with great splendor and majesty.

"You may want to open your eyes and see the sun rising," Samuel remarked.

Danny was oscillating between wakefulness and slumber, but in that instant heard Samuel speaking and opened his eyes. At first, he watched the sun with a dull and resigned spirit but gradually the image took him by surprise. He had never seen the sun so big and near and so majestic and free. And yet, at the same time it appeared to him aloof and indifferent. He gazed at it with inexplicable fascination, as if he was seeing it for the first time. A painful and overwhelming sensation and yearning for death gripped him.

"If the sun exists with sovereignty, without being dependent on any earthly life," he thought, "all should be well after death."

"Can you try to walk slowly?" he heard Samuel asking.

"Yes, I can," he replied with almost inaudible voice.

Samuel helped Danny get up and they walked slowly forwards. Each step was a painful effort. Besides the physical exhaustion, now his mouth tasted bitter and he could hear a continuous and irritating noise in his ears.

Moreover, he was haunted by an acute sensation of guilt and anxiety.

After they had travelled for about two hours, they found a narrow and dusty path stretching along one side of the river and almost parallel to it. It appeared to originate from the main dirt road. They had hardly joined this path when Samuel saw the fading footprints of a soldier's boots crossing the path, going towards the river.

"These are fresh footprints. Perhaps, from the previous evening or even from early this morning. I wonder where the soldier was coming from and where he was going. Perhaps, he was coming from Dolo and going to God knows where. Obviously, he has crossed the river. Can you imagine what sort of a soldier he was? From the length of his stride, I would say that he wasn't a wounded soldier."

Samuel followed the footprints up to the river's edge and concluded that the soldier had indeed crossed the river, but he himself did not wish to cross the river and pursue the footprints any further. They left the footprints behind them and advanced. As the sun rose slowly over the eastern horizon, it became warmer and Danny felt better and found walking tolerable. Samuel, too, became cheerful and talkative.

"My old man loves to travel to strange places," he told Danny for the second time. "I too love to travel now, but in the beginning, when I was still young, I didn't like it that much. When you travel, you realize what a great and wonderful place this earth of ours is and what a great privilege it is to be entrusted with it."

"But there isn't much to see here, only this dry red dust stretching endlessly before and after us and this dusty and ugly river," Danny countered morosely.

"The river is our lifeline. If you only knew what it means not to have this river for a day or two," Samuel chuckled good-naturedly. "Besides, not all places are dull like this place. In the north there are chains of majestic mountains spreading uninterrupted for hundreds of kilometers and impressive valleys and gorges. In the west there are tall and proud trees standing erect with their leafy and spreading branches, undisturbed since the beginning of time. If you cross the Ganale and travel some distance north and eastwards, you will come to places where wonderful wild animals freely roam."

Danny too would have loved to travel to the ends of the earth had he not been sickly and helpless. He would have loved to travel as far as his feet could carry him, without ever wishing to return or look back. When he was in Neghelle and had seen the cross-country busses leaving for

Addis, he had always felt painfully jealous of the people who were inside them. He even felt jealous of the soldiers who left the town in densely packed military trucks, even though he knew that most of them would never return to the city and to their families alive.

"Has your prophet a family of his own?" he asked Samuel.

"If you mean whether he's married and all that, my answer is no."

"Why hasn't he married and had his own children?"

"Because he was not called to that."

"How can he be happy in life by merely travelling from one place to another?"

"If you think one's happiness rests in marriage and family alone, you're mistaken. The prophet is persuaded that the fulfilment of his life and that of mine lies in helping others discover the purpose of their life and not as such in fulfilling any earthly duties."

"What does he mean?"

"It's hard to explain to a person of your age."

"Why, you're not much older than I! How old are you?"

"I'm sixteen."

"Well, I'm fourteen."

"I'm just explaining to you what the prophet believes."

"What do you want to be when you grow up, a prophet?"

"One doesn't become a prophet because one wishes to be one," responds Samuel smiling. "One is called to it. Believe me, it's not something you want to become."

"What's your dream then?"

"I don't know yet what I wish to become. The prophet says that everything will become apparent to me when the right time comes."

"You are lucky; you've a future to look forward to. As for me, my future grows more uncertain with every passing day," said Danny sorrowfully.

"Now you're talking openly and you're not afraid to confront the issue. You're dying, aren't you?"

Danny did not reply.

"You may have some reason to believe that the future contains nothing but suffering for you, but you can never tell what life has in store for you."

"What do you know about life and the future?"

"I know as much as the next person."

"You've no idea what I've been going through. How many times I have been lied to, have hoped against all hopes, and been disappointed. The future contains nothing but death and destruction."

"You may say so of your perishing body. But it's difficult to say likewise of your soul. Suffering and death alone don't destroy the soul."

"Oh!" Danny groaned. "Please, stop preaching to me!"

"My old man once told me that what makes a human being truly great is his capacity to resist suffering from destroying the soul."

"Blast your prophet!"

"You don't need to be blasphemous just because you're suffering. Other people also suffer, you know."

They were silent for some time and then Danny put in the next question.

"But what did he mean?"

Samuel understood what he was referring to.

"The tendency of suffering is to destroy. It certainly destroys the physical body. As to our soul, our will must first give in for suffering to destroy the soul."

"How can I think of being great when I'm totally helpless and my daily existence depends on others?" Danny asked trying to suppress his anger.

"Why do you resent so much being dependent on others? We all are dependent on others to a certain extent, if you think about it."

"It's shameful to be dependent on others indefinitely, which is why I resent it."

"We develop character in our dependency. The one who helps learns how to be compassionate and gracious and the one who is being helped learns how to be humble and grateful. My old man and I have been dependent on others many times and others have been dependent on us, too. This is how we learn to be real human beings; this is how we fulfil our earthly duties."

"I was always receiving and never giving. That hurts a lot. Our life is like being in children's marketplace, if you think about it. The game is enjoyable only when we buy as much as we sell. There is no greatness in being always on the receiving end."

"Your life just started. A time may come when you will give, if giving really delights you."

"Which life?" Danny burst in anger. "What future are you talking about? You have no idea about the things you talk."

"The prophet once taught that," Samuel continued calmly, "with greatness, it's like when a woman becomes pregnant with a child. From her body she knows that life has taken root in her and is developing. When the spirit of greatness takes root in you, you shall know of it. No one needs to tell you anything about it."

"True greatness is indifference, my father believed, indifference to power, to praise, to reward."

"That's certainly one type of greatness," Samuel consented. "But it's not the only type."

"What's greatness to you?"

Samuel thought briefly and replied: "Meekness. Meekness is endless."

Danny wanted to change the subject.

"Wasn't there anything or anyone you missed when you lived and travelled with your prophet?"

"Oh, yes, I missed many things."

"What did you miss most?"

"Playing with children," Samuel answered instinctively. "We spent much of the time with adults, you know. I'm ashamed to confess it, but adults aren't the most exciting beings to be with, even though it's not their fault they're adults."

"What else did you miss?"

"Well, it all depends on the time and the place. Sometimes this, sometimes that."

"Did you miss your real family, your mother and father?"

"I never knew them very well, you see. Besides, I was accustomed to being with the prophet."

"Is your prophet a lonely man?"

"Not at all."

"He must be a busy man then."

"Sometimes. There were days when we avoided people. But there were also days, and sometimes days and nights, when we were engulfed by crowds of people. Some of the people who sought the counsel of the prophet were highly respected in the land."

"No one is too highly respected," Danny retorted with vexation, "when it comes to seeking the counsel of a prophet or a wise man."

"What do you mean?"

"One should first acknowledge one's insignificance before seeking the help of another. I've seen a multitude of the so-called great people prostrating themselves before the so-called wise men, to be healed, to get rich, to be spared of this or that calamity."

"But not all the people who come to a prophet are selfish. Not all people who prostrate themselves before a higher being are cowardly."

"Human beings are despicable. They cannot be great as long as they're needy. And we all are needy in one way or another. We don't admit it because we're proud."

"There's an earthly weakness and a heavenly weakness. You mustn't mistake the two."

"I don't see the difference between the two."

"You will, one day."

They travelled the remaining distance in silence, until they had felt the strength of the sun. Then Samuel suggested taking a long break. They found a dry and shaded area not far from the river bank and decided to spend the remainder of the day there. Samuel took out four of the military biscuits and offered Danny two of them.

"We shall keep the fish for later. These should be sufficient for now."

After he ate the biscuits Danny fell asleep instantly, but fifteen minutes later he was attacked by another round of ceaseless and dry coughing which lasted for a long time. This time he threw up all the food he had eaten that day and the previous day and spat blood continuously. The boy became very weak and his skin turned very pale. Samuel poured water on his face in order to keep him awake but Danny eventually slipped into unconsciousness. The cough and the spitting ceased and the boy collapsed, apparently, lifeless, on the ground. Samuel knelt down next to him, uncovered his chest, and put his right ear on his left chest, trying to ascertain that his heart was still beating. He could not hear his heart beating.

Samuel rose to his feet and unfurled his hands in despair, tears rolling down his cheeks and his lips trembling uncontrollably. He knelt once again beside Danny and studied him closely, with his sight now blurred with tears. He whispered Danny's name repeatedly, but Danny lay lifeless. At long last, he carefully wrapped him, or what was left of him, with his father's military jacket, meaning to bury him, and laid him under a bush. He himself went to the river to bathe, weary and distraught.

Chapter 7

After he had bathed, he sat by the riverbank feeling forlorn and having lost the desire to undertake anything. Then he suddenly felt a shadow resting over his head and he looked up. In front of him was standing a young girl, clad in a dark-red and black *guntino* and a long, brilliant amber necklace. Her jet-black hair was braided and richly decorated with amber and her naked arms were adorned with henna. She was wearing a pair of sandals made of goat skin.

Samuel stood up, not trusting his own eyes.

"The wilderness can be elusive sometimes, you mustn't forget," he remembered his old man once warning him. "Particularly, when you're in great distress or suffering from sleeplessness or scorched by thirst. In those situations, your mind produces all sorts of images, which appear so authentic that you have a hard time believing they are unreal."

"I was watching you," the girl began meanwhile in accented Amharic, looking at him with frank and merry eyes. "You look very sad."

Her voice was sweet.

"Who are you?"

"Did I frighten you?" she chuckled good-naturedly.

"Can I touch you?" he asked her foolishly and, involuntarily stretching out his hand, he touched her bare arm.

"Do you think I am a phantom?" she laughed.

"What on earth are you doing in the wilderness all by yourself, or are you with someone?"

"What are you doing here yourself?"

"Are you real or am I just imagining you? I must be imagining because I'm sad and feel terribly lonely."

"You're not imagining anything. It's broad daylight and you've touched me. I don't blame you if you have difficulty in believing that I'm real. It's not usual for a girl of my age to be alone in a place like this."

"So, you're alone?"

Samuel regarded the girl, terrified that she might disappear from his sight at any moment.

"Do you have something to eat?" the girl asked him.

Perplexed, he looked left and right.

"I must have some grilled fish in my bag."

"I'm ashamed to beg, but I'm hungry."

He hesitated to reply or even to move.

"I must be hearing the voice I'm desperate to hear," he thought.

"You're not dreaming or hallucinating. I am real." The girl reassured him, as if reading his mind.

"What's your name, what are you doing here in the wilderness?"

"My name is Roi. I'm here searching for a tree that has the power to heal my brother."

"What sort of a tree?"

"It's called the Tree of Strength."

"The Tree of Strength?"

"That's right. I must bring it to my mother, otherwise, my brother will soon die."

"What tree of strength can you find in this desolate place?"

"A prophet once told my mother to seek for the Tree of Strength in this region. He said my brother lacked the will to live and seeing the Tree of Strength would restore his will. He said the tree is his only hope."

"What prophet?" he asked her, for once forgetting his doubt about the girl standing in front of him.

"My mother said she met him one afternoon as she was fetching water at a well outside our village."

"When was that?"

"A long time ago."

"Can you remember when, please? It's very important to me."

"Why is it important to you? A while ago you were doubting my existence. Anyway, I don't remember the exact time, but it must be a long time ago."

"But how long? Please try to remember."

"You should ask my mother."

"So has your mother been seeking the tree ever since?"

"Not really. At first, she didn't even believe in it. Then when she spoke about it, nobody in our family believed her story. They said she was making things up because she was desperate. So, she ignored it. But of late, my brother's condition has growing worse and my mother can't stop thinking about the Tree of Strength. Then one day she saw the prophet in a dream urging her to seek the Tree of Strength."

"How did she know he was a prophet?"

"He told her so."

"You must be telling the truth. You can't be making this up," Samuel said, fixing his eyes on the girl.

"Why shouldn't I tell the truth?"

"Where is your mother, can I talk to her?"

"My mother is at home."

"Which village or town are you from? Do you live nearby? I need help."

"What help?"

"I and my friend were crossing the wilderness when he was attacked by a vicious coughing fit. He now lies dead. I was about to bury him when you came."

"Where is he, can I see him?"

"Are you sure?"

"I've seen a dead body before." Roi shrugged her shoulders.

He pointed towards the tree and silently led her to Danny. The girl approached the lifeless body and cautiously squatted in front of it.

"Are you certain he's dead?" she asked Samuel without taking her eyes off Danny.

"I'm afraid so, yes."

"Strange, my brother sometimes looks exactly like this."

"You mean so lifeless? Without breathing and all?"

"Very pale and bloodless."

"What is his illness?"

"He suffers from terrible seizures," Roi replied still squatting down but lifting up her head towards Samuel.

"In the beginning they occurred at long intervals, once a

month or so, but these days they come frequently, almost every third or fourth day, and each time he suffers greatly.”

“Where's your father?”

“I have no father. My father left us a long time ago, when I was still a child.”

They were silent for a moment, and then the girl stood up.

“Does your family live nearby? Can I give him a proper burial where you and your family live?”

“Why don't you bury him here? What difference does it make where he's buried?”

“I suppose it doesn't make any difference.”

“I can't help you. I must leave now and mind my own business, otherwise, it'll be too late.”

“Please don't go yet,” Samuel begged her. “I'm awfully sad and lonely.”

“I can't stay any longer.”

“Can I come with you?”

“Where?”

“Can I accompany you some distance?”

“How about him?”

“I don't want to bury him yet. I shall wait until the sun sets and then I will bury him.”

“I see. Come along then.”

Roi turned to leave and Samuel followed her.

"How do you know where to look for the tree? Do you know what the tree looks like?"

"The prophet told my mother to search for the tree in a valley where there is a big red rock and a small river flows."

"But the wilderness is full of valleys and red rocks and the river crosses the wilderness from one end to the other."

"Are you trying to discourage me?"

"By no means."

"If the man was a prophet indeed, do you think he would tell my mother to search for something without intending to help her along the way? I believe there will be more hints and clues if I obey and take the first step."

"Your faith is great. How do you know which tree you should be looking for?"

"I like to think that I'll know the tree when I see it."

"How could your mother allow you to undertake such a perilous journey into the wilderness alone?"

"You ask too many questions. My mother didn't send me, to begin with. I decided to come here by myself. How could I stand by while my brother was dying, when I could do something for him? To risk my life to find a tree that may not exist may sound foolishness to you, but it doesn't to me, not anymore. You may say: Even if the tree exists, there is no guarantee that it has the power to heal. That may well be. But it's also cowardice not to take a risk, not to try. There are so many things, so many unknowns, in life which we haven't tried, don't you agree?"

"You've spoken wisely. You must have thought about this for a long time."

"There isn't anything particularly wise in my statement, if you think about it. I've lived with the problem all my life, waiting for something extraordinary to happen, but doing nothing. We tried all the usual remedies and they all failed us. This is the only unusual thing I've done; the only risk I have taken to try to save my brother."

"I can't imagine how much your poor mother is worrying right now."

"My brother's problem aside, I've been longing to do something unusual all my life. I've felt myself enchained and helpless. At the same time, I've always felt an extraordinary energy within me. My mother and I lived in great anxiety and expectation, you should understand. When I first heard my mother speaking about the prophet, I scolded her and told her to forget about it. I thought it was wishful thinking. I didn't want her, didn't want us, to be deceived. I was afraid of building our hope on something that has no firm foundation, no life of its own. But I couldn't get it out of my mind all the same, I couldn't forget it. I didn't think about it every day, but it was there, at the back of my mind, all along."

"You are not an illusion. You are real. You speak as a normal human being." Samuel concluded.

"Still doubting my existence?" Roi looked at him reproachfully and increased her pace.

"Where did you learn to speak Amharic? I see that you're a Somali girl."

"My entire clan speaks Amharic," was her reply.

"Where does your clan dwell?"

"My clan dwells in its own village."

"Wait, didn't you ask for something to eat? I nearly forgot."

"Go and get it then."

He hesitated. He was almost sure that he would never see her again if he went back to bring the fish.

"Well?" she challenged him.

He went back and returned with the fish. She was waiting for him. The girl ate at leisure.

"When was the last time you had anything to eat?" he asked her.

"This morning."

"What did you eat? Did you bring something with you from home?"

"I'm sure you didn't bring anything with you when you fled into the wilderness, did you? How long would it have last had I brought something with me? I can't make a journey into a wilderness reliant on the things I bring from home."

"But you didn't answer my question."

"I discovered a hive and wild honey this morning."

"Here, drink." Samuel offered her his water bottle and she took it thankfully.

"How long will you search for the tree?"

"I will not return home until I have found it."

When she finished eating, Roi resumed her journey and Samuel walked alongside.

"Are you sure you want to leave your friend behind?" she asked him.

"I'm torn between two thoughts. I want to accompany you in your quest for the tree, but I don't want to give up on Danny. I find it impossible to accept that he's dead. Even though he was a dying boy and I met him only a few days ago, his image is vividly imprinted in my memory as if I've known him for a long time. Even now as I'm speaking to you, I hear his voice in my mind. Danny is his name, by the way."

"So, do you believe in the existence of the Tree of Strength?"

"I believe you."

"But you haven't answered my question."

"I believe your mother."

"That she has met the prophet?"

"Yes."

"And the prophet, do you believe him?"

"I do."

"Are you in earnest?" Roi screamed.

"I am in earnest."

Roi stopped and stared at Samuel. Her beautiful and childish face suddenly became pale, her eyes looked bigger and immobile, and her lips trembled slightly.

"You were having doubts about the tree, admit it!" he challenged her.

Her beautiful eyes were suddenly filled with tears, but she remained stubbornly silent.

"You're on a dangerous quest, Roi, but I believe the Tree of Strength exists, only I don't know where it exists," he told her with almost inaudible voice.

At that instant, they heard someone coughing, a weak cough, but unmistakable, and they both stopped to listen.

"Did you hear that?" Samuel asked Roi, not trusting his own ears.

"A cough," she said softly.

They looked back and waited, pricking their ears. Then they heard the cough once more.

"He's back!" Samuel screamed with delight and rushed to Danny.

Chapter 8

When Samuel arrived, he found Danny still lying immobile but with his ghostly eyes opened. He knelt beside Danny and felt his face with his right palm. His face was corpse-cold but Samuel was certain that Danny was alive.

"Oh, I'm so glad you came back," he whispered, fresh tears suddenly rolling down his cheeks.

He glanced backward over his shoulder to tell Roi how glad he felt, but Roi was no longer standing behind or beside him. He stood up, suddenly filled with anxiety, and looked around, but she was nowhere to be seen. Almost sure that she had disappeared, he went forward and called her name aloud. There was no response.

"Have I really been hallucinating all this time or was she a phantom, as she said?" He wondered and returned to Danny.

For two days Danny made no appreciable movement nor uttered a word. Samuel kept him in the shade during the day and burnt twigs at night to keep him warm. But apart from rinsing his lips with water he could not feed him any food. During what seemed an interminable period of time, Samuel hoped with great expectation and yearning to see the image of Roi or to hear her sweet voice emerging from somewhere, but there was no Roi. Indeed, the silence of the wilderness was so disturbing and intolerable to him that he went frequently to the river to hear the sound of his own splashing in the water.

Towards midday on the third day Danny woke up from a long and undisturbed sleep and raised himself up to a sitting position. Samuel was sitting at some distance, two or three meters away from Danny, his face towards the river and gently rocking his body rhythmically back and forth and chanting something to himself. Somehow, he perceived that Danny was awake, but took time to finish his chanting. Then he slowly turned his entire body towards Danny and looked at him with a weary smile on his face.

"You're awake," he said.

The voice, however, was not his usual cheerful voice. It sounded like the voice of an adult who was accustomed to worry and care.

"What happened?" Danny asked, faintly aware that he had gone through something calamitous.

"You fought with death himself for three days, and, as it turns out, you have overcome."

Samuel's eyes were unusually small and red, but still lively. His face seemed to have aged.

They stayed at the same place until the next morning, waiting for Danny to sufficiently recover for travel. Samuel could not catch fish because there were alligators in the river. He went to different places and stayed out a long time fishing, thinking of Roi much of the time. Many times, he was tempted to tell Danny about Roi but decided against it. The time was unpropitious, he thought. He was cautious not to say anything that might cause Danny confusion or alarm.

Danny was relieved to some extent at being left alone, because he regretted being dependent on Samuel, even though his primary purpose in running away from his mother had been to free himself from over-dependency on her.

Very early on the fifth day since they had left Dolo the boys recommenced their journey and managed to travel for nearly four hours with only two breaks. The rest of the day they spent resting and sleeping.

Towards three o'clock in the afternoon, while Danny was still sleeping, Samuel went to the river fishing. When Danny awoke, the sun was about to descend towards the western horizon but Samuel had not yet returned. He decided to collect twigs for a fire to grill the fish in case Samuel had been successful. On his way, however, Danny heard Samuel calling his name and returned to the place where they had taken rest. Samuel was standing next to the river, carrying two bundles of fish in his hands.

"We should resume our journey," he urged. "I'm sure you've had enough rest."

"Shouldn't we grill the fish first?"

"If we do, it'll be too dark to set out again today."

"Why catch so many fish if you intend to continue our journey tonight?"

"We may not be able to find fish at our next stopover. These are not too heavy to carry."

So, they set off for the second time that day and travelled, nonetheless, in the dark, always parallel to the river, for nearly three hours.

From that day on, they travelled daily, twice a day, in the morning for about three hours and in the evening for two. And from that day on, Danny's health remained, by and large, stable. Indeed, he was never to be attacked by the same rough cough or spit blood ever again.

Chapter 9

On the tenth day since they had left Dolo, they came to a place where the river formed a big oval pool in which Samuel decided to swim. After he had carefully inspected the surrounding area, he grinned with satisfaction and put down his staff and bag at the edge of the river.

"The river and its banks are clear of weeds, which is a good indication that there are no alligators lurking inside. But the water is still murky and we should be very careful."

He removed a grilled fish from his bag and placed it at the upper opening of the pool and watched it float. The fish glided towards the other end, but no alligator emerged to claim it. Sitting on the riverbank, Samuel let his feet dangle inside the river and encouraged Danny to do the same.

Danny very much wanted to, but was afraid lest his cough return.

"Come on, have some faith. Your cough is gone for good, I'm certain of it," Samuel told him, his voice resonating with laughter.

The day was hot and windless as usual. After hesitating for some seconds, Danny finally decided to try it. Sitting next to Samuel, he cautiously put his feet inside the water. His heart began to pound very fast as he felt the coldness of the water. Excitement and anxiety gripped him with equal force and his body began to tremble. So, he withdrew his feet.

"It's all right, put them back into the water."

Danny put his feet back into the water and this time kept them there. It took a long time for his heartbeat to settle to a normal pace, during which time he was unable to tell whether he was enjoying the cold sensation of the water or not. Samuel gently splashed the water with his feet and whistled nonchalantly, studying Danny with a cheerful and challenging look.

"Do you wish to learn how to swim?"

"You mean now?"

"Yes, why not?"

"I know how to swim, I mean, theoretically."

"So, do you want to try?"

Danny's heart began to beat wildly once again, and once again he was gripped by the opposing forces of excitement and anxiety. Samuel, in the meantime, had undressed and entered the river and was swimming back and forth between the riverbanks.

Danny remembered what good a swimmer his father had been. He had seen him swim many times in dangerous rivers and lakes. But he had never tried to teach him how to swim, partly because he was always ill, but partly because his father had never cared really. Many of the boys he had befriended at school could swim. He had accompanied them to nearby rivers and *elas* and watched them swim with painful envy. The boys had grown accustomed to counting on him as their watchman, someone to look out for the adults when they swam in forbidden waters or at forbidden times.

"All you need to do is to perform simple mechanical movements," Samuel told him standing in front of him and demonstrating the movements with his hands and legs. "The secret of swimming is to keep on moving and to breathe normally. You sink when you stop moving and you get tired when you stop breathing."

"I'll learn some other time, but not today," Danny countered decisively.

"As you wish."

Samuel returned to the river and swam diagonally back and forth and tested his strength by swimming against the current. Danny contented himself with keeping his feet inside the water and feeling the mixed sensation of anxiety and delight. The longer he stayed, however, the more the sensation of delight prevailed and for the first time in many, many days, he was tempted to believe in the existence of another side of life which was at once exciting and peaceful.

Nevertheless, that same night his mind was filled with the experiences of the day, so much so that he felt restless and was unable to fall asleep. He was tormented by the thought that he had been deprived of a great joy by not being able to swim. The realization was exceptionally painful considering his unreserved love for and emotional response to the sight of water. This pain was not new but that night he was acutely conscious of it.

The following day, they set off early in the morning as usual and travelled for two hours. They travelled in silence, desirous to put as many miles behind them as possible. Despite the short sleep he had had, Danny kept up with Samuel with a relative ease. During the break, Samuel announced that he was feeling tired and wished to take a nap before he went fishing. Danny, on the other hand, still felt restless and wished to occupy himself. Sitting beside Samuel and staring at the river he could not stop thinking about swimming. He waited until Samuel had fallen asleep and, then, cautiously stood up and went to the river, his heart suddenly beating fast. He was filled with anxiety.

Standing at the river, he looked at it with extreme fascination, as if he was seeing the brown god for the first time. As his eyes remained fixed on the river, he gradually ceased to look at it and succumbed to the pressing desire to jump into it and swim. In a very short time, this desire not only became inordinate but also prevailed over all his other desires and fears. The river was flowing silently but Danny had no doubt of its speed and power. He remembered Samuel telling him to cross a fast-flowing river by always swimming diagonally.

He slowly took off his clothes, all the while staring at the river, as if in a trance, his heart pounding fearfully and his arms tightly crossed over his chest. At long last, he cautiously stepped into the water and stood in the river and felt the pressure of the flowing water. He stood there for a while, uncertain of his next step, but was unable to bear the excitement and the uncertainty. He gently leaned forward, stretched his arms out straight in front of him and threw himself into the water, with his eyes closed and his chin turned up. Before he could make any further movement, however, the river tossed him viciously into the middle and swirled around him, drawing him downwards.

He tried to make the simple movements Samuel had shown him but the river gave him no time for all of that. Almost instantly, he lost all sense of orientation and kept making frantic and wild movements with his hands, trying, at the same time, to keep his mouth shut. But he was unable to do so. Suffering from an excruciating pain in his chest, he was unable to resist opening his mouth for a brief moment. In that instant, water gushed into his mouth forcefully and he began to sink deep into the river. Had his desperate and lonely struggle continued for a few more seconds, he would have given up. But Samuel, who nearly lost his own life in the attempt, came to his aid. It so happened that he suddenly woke up "with an urgent sensation" that Danny was up to "something terribly dangerous". When he arrived at the river, Danny was being swiftly carried away by the river, his face turned downwards, and feebly trying to stay afloat. Samuel sprinted ahead in order to "overtake" the river before diving in fully clothed. After repeated failures and exasperation, he finally succeeded in hauling Danny back to dry land.

Once out of the river, it became apparent that Danny had lost consciousness. Samuel prostrated him on the ground on his back and repeatedly pressed on his stomach to expel the water Danny had swallowed. Indeed, Danny choked and spat out plenty of water. Then Samuel wrapped him tightly with his father's military jacket and let him lie down in the shade. Throughout the remainder of the day and the night his condition remained stable. The next morning, he awoke on his own and asked for something to eat. Samuel gave him dry biscuits and a piece of grilled fish, which he ate with appetite. When he had finished, he stood up and expressed his readiness for the journey. Samuel, however, suggested remaining another day in the same location, so that Danny could fully recover.
"I had an uneasy sleep and a bad dream last night," Samuel declared.
"I'm sorry. I was the cause of it all."
"You gave me quite a fright yesterday."
"Were you afraid that I was dying?"
"You were nearly gone. It was reckless of you to go into the water unattended. You should have trusted me when I said I could teach you."
"I couldn't resist the temptation."
"Suppose you'd drowned?"

"So, what if I had drowned? Nobody would miss me. I mean, except you, of course. Even you would eventually accept my death and march on through the wilderness all alone. You must admit that your journey would be faster without me."

"How about your poor mother?"

"I'm sure by now she's convinced that I was killed during the jet attack."

"Are you really so indifferent to your own life?"

"I didn't say that."

They were silent briefly but Danny put up the next question.

"Do you believe in dreams?"

"Sometimes, yes. You don't?"

"There's not a single night when I haven't had nightmares and bad dreams."

"There was a time in my life when I used to suffer from bad dreams."

"So, what was your last dream about?"

"In my dream, you were jumping into the river for the second time. This time, however, there were alligators inside the river."

"Did you save me?" Danny asked him eagerly.

"I woke up before I could save you. The alligators encircled you as soon as the water had drawn you into the middle. I don't know where they came from. They were many in number and they looked furious. But they did not rush to tear you apart. Somehow the river wasn't carrying you away. It was as if you were floating in a lake. The alligators approached you slowly, gnashing green and irregular teeth. But before they could seize you, the water suddenly sucked you downwards in a rapid and unending spiral. At that point, I arrived and extended my staff for you to hold on to, but you were too far away from me."

"What good was it to hold on to your staff when I was surrounded by alligators?"

"I was asking the same question myself, but I was desperate."

"Did I die finally?"

"You were face down and you were immobile, but I couldn't tell whether you were dead or alive. I suppose you were alive."

"Strange. I also had a dream but this time it wasn't a bad dream for a change. In my dream I entered the water for the second time, but the dream ended differently."

"Really?"

"Yes."

"What happened, how did your dream end?"

"There were no alligators in my dream and the water wasn't as furious as yesterday."

Samuel looked at Danny eagerly.

"Tell me what happened next?" There was urgency in his voice.

"I swam. I crossed the river peacefully and crisscrossed it many times."

"You had that dream because you're very eager to swim."

"May be. But which dream is correct, mine or yours?"

"A dream is neither correct nor incorrect. It may be a warning or an encouragement. It all depends on what you make of it."

"But what does that mean?"

"You must listen to your own heart. But you mustn't be overconfident or negligent."

"What does your dream mean, can you explain it to me?" Danny asked him anxiously.

"I'm not gifted at interpreting dreams. But we must agree on one thing. You should be very careful. You may be thinking that you've missed out on a lot by not being able to swim. But swimming is not very important. Even dogs and donkeys can swim. You'll be able to swim when the right time comes. The prophet used to say, life is more precious than action."

"Action suggests life, I know this more than anybody else," Danny countered. "Many of the boys in my class could swim when they were much younger."

"Listen, if you wish to learn how to swim, we should wait until we have found a place where the river makes a big pool. There it flows slower and you have room to swim. Don't try to learn by yourself. I can teach you easily and safely."
Danny nodded in agreement.

Chapter 10

The next day they set off very early in the morning. Samuel wanted to cover as much distance as possible that day as he was worried about the spreading of the war. Danny understood and cooperated. He had been haunted by guilt for having held Samuel back so often and for so long. Except for occasional exchanges of the water bottle, they walked in silence much of the day and relatively faster.

After they had travelled for about four hours, they took a break around nine o'clock in the morning and Samuel decided to go fishing. He said he was not feeling tired. Seeing that Danny was exhausted, he advised him to rest. Danny agreed and lay down, intending to take a nap. Indeed, he fell asleep almost immediately but woke up ten minutes later, his mind being alert and agitated.

Throughout the morning his mind had been filled with the impression of his dream from the previous night and the incident at the river. Now the more he thought about his dream the stronger became his desire to go and try swimming in the river. At last, he opened his eyes and tried to think of different things but none of them were appealing to him. He got up and walked back and forth like a lion in a cage. His heart was beating faster and his palms were palpitating. The anxiety and excitement which had taken hold of him yesterday filled his whole being once again.

"There's no use trying to escape from my fate," he murmured. "I must go and confront the lion in his den."

As if drawn by an invisible and irresistible hand, he walked slowly towards the river, taking the direction opposite to the one Samuel had taken. Was he under the influence of a secret death wish? he thought briefly. When he reached the river, he stood at the edge in great alertness, intently staring at the flowing brown water for a long time, as though it was a deadly snake which could jump up at any time to bite him.

At long last he removed his clothes slowly and cautiously put his feet into the water, just like he had done the day before yesterday. His entire body was now shaking uncontrollably with anxiety as well as excitement. He closed his eyes and threw his body forward into the water. The river received him with a powerful forward thrust. After a fleeting panic and struggle, he was able to coordinate his movements and to keep his body afloat. He swam diagonally to the other side and came out of the river intact.

In the subsequent days Danny was filled with extraordinary exuberance, and the travel in the wilderness ceased to weary him. The boys travelled as usual for the next three days. During the intermediate break, Danny spent the day mostly in the river, swimming. It seemed as if he could not get enough of swimming and the cold sensation of the water. Samuel too was caught up in Danny's exuberance and spent long hours in the river every day.

Chapter 11

One morning, they were passing by three big red rocks surrounded by shrubs and decided to take a break there. Suddenly, they heard the bleating of goats nearby. When they looked around, they saw a handful of goats in the bushes, about a stone's throw away from them, a little to their left, peacefully grazing. Samuel ducked down and signaled to Danny to do the same. They moved cautiously away from the river towards the bushes, hid behind one of the rocks and studied their surroundings. Except for the goats they could not see anyone.

"What do you think, have we been sighted already?" Danny whispered with a mixed emotion of excitement and fear.

"If there's a shepherd tending the goats, he must've seen us," Samuel whispered back.

They waited in silence but nothing happened. They could not see anyone.

"What do you think, should we reveal ourselves?" Danny inquired.

"I'm not sure. The people living in this area are Somalis. Who knows, they may identify with their kin on the other side. We should be careful."

"These people are Gerimeros," Danny corrected Samuel. "The Somalis on the other side are Hawiyas. The Gerimeros have no fellowship with the Hawiyas, because the Hawiyas despise them. They consider them as their inferiors."

"How do you know?"

"Never mind, I know.

"But how?"

"My mother is a Gerimero."

"Really?"

Danny nodded.

"Do you think we'll safe if we reveal ourselves?"

"I think so. I can talk to them."

"Do you speak their tongue?"

"Yes, I do."

Samuel hesitated.

"But I'm not sure."

"Why not?"

"I suggest we move on cautiously and rest somewhere else. If we're discovered, that's a different matter."

"If they catch us sneaking around, they may not think of us as innocent and desperate boys who are trying to save their lives. They may be suspicious of us. But if we go to them of our own free will and explain our situation to them, they may feel sorry for us and help us. They may give us food and drink and invite us to stay a couple of days with them. They may advise us which way to take and even send us with a message to the next village, so that we'll be welcomed and supported in everything we need for our journey."

"Aren't you getting a little carried away?"

"What makes you think that?"

Samuel sighed deeply.

"The turn of events may take an alternative direction. We're putting our lives at risk if we act injudiciously. I suggest we leave these people alone and continue with our journey. We've been doing fine up to now."

"But these people may give us some decent food and let us rest for some days. My feet are hurting and I detest eating fish all the time."

"But we'd be putting ourselves in a position of great uncertainty if we expose ourselves to people we don't know. It's a time of war, you mustn't forget. These people may not like the Somalis on the other side, but they may not like us either."

"Why shouldn't they like us? What reason do they have?"

"They may not want our interference."

"But why?"

"They may want to be left alone."

"You're not making any sense."

"Suppose they become suspicious of us? Suppose they take us for informers or spies?"

"What?"

"It's not that hard to explain. Just think of it. Neither of us is from this area, but you speak their language. These people live near a hostile border. The soldiers on either side of the border don't trust them because each side thinks that they're loyal to the other side. So, when they suddenly see two strange boys coming out of nowhere, they'll think that the Ethiopian soldiers have sent them to spy on them. Nobody will believe our story."

Danny was thoughtful for a moment.

"At least we should find out where the goats come from and how many there are," he suggested, presently.

"Why?"

"Knowledge is a weapon; don't you think?"

"Leave the goats in peace."

"We can steal one of them."

"Excuse me! What for?"

"To slaughter and eat it, of course, what else for?"

"Are you out of your mind? We should leave this place at once!" exclaimed Samuel emphatically.

"Calm down, will you? Nobody'll get hurt if we steal one goat. I'm sure these people have enough to eat. We, on the other hand, haven't eaten a decent meal for many days."

"We've been provided for so far. Have some faith."

"I'm weary of eating fish every day."

"You are seeking an excuse to steal from them. The truth is, if you're seeking an occasion to do something bad, you'll always find a good excuse. But you should also bear in mind that others may equally find sufficient reasons to do us injustice."

"My, Samuel, you're quite the philosopher, aren't you!"

"We should leave the goats in peace and mind our own business."

"What's one goat to these people?"

Samuel was puzzled by Danny's unusual and sudden defiance, but he did not wish to dispute with him any further. Meanwhile, Danny cautiously left their hiding place and went to the other side of the bushes and looked carefully around. There was no one around except the goats. He counted eleven goats, four of which were kids.

"Okay, if we steal a goat now, in a broad daylight, someone will most likely find out. Besides, we don't know where their owners live. Their village may be on our way. We should first find a hiding place by the river and rest there for the rest of the day. Someone must come and collect the goats at some point. We'll follow him and find out where the goats stay. In the evening, when everybody's gone to bed, we'll steal one of the goats."

"Suppose they keep their goats inside their huts? They'd be foolish to keep them outside."

"Many in Neghelle keep their cattle outside in a stable."

"But this is not Neghelle. Here the hyenas roam about freely."

"But we haven't encountered any hyenas so far."

"That doesn't mean they don't exist."

"You're not up for an adventure, Samuel, what's the matter with you?"

"I ask you, what is the matter with you?"

Samuel looked confused and frustrated. He turned his face away and kept quiet.

"Okay, I've another idea!" retorted Danny in a stifled voice.

Samuel did not react.

"How about we steal one of the goats now and keep it with us until it's evening."

"You're most certainly out of your mind."

"I'm not out of my mind. But I'm fed up with eating fish."

"Suppose the goat bleats?"

"We shall muzzle its mouth. I know how to muzzle a goat."

"Just think what you're suggesting," Samuel said with some impatience. "There are not hundreds of goats. Just eleven! The owners will immediately know if one of their goats is missing. It's precious to them. No matter how late they'll discover, they'll not give up their goat for lost. Remember, this is a time of war. Losing a goat means a lot to them."

"In a Somali community, domestic animals, including camels, are tended by women or children, mostly by children. The men don't meddle in this business. I know this very well. If we're courageous, we'll get away with it easily. Trust me."

With great persistence Samuel tried to talk Danny out of it but Danny was bent on executing his plan. They found that one of the rocks had a cave-like structure facing the river and decided to hide and rest there.

"I'll go out and spy the surrounding area one more time," said Danny scanning the cave with satisfaction. "Then, I'll snatch one goat and bring it here."

"I'll come with you."

They agreed first to survey the place, each one heading out in the opposite direction to the other and returning to the cave before attempting to steal a goat. They went out leaving their belongings behind. After ten minutes or so, first Samuel returned, while Danny took longer. Samuel was about to go out for the second time when he saw Danny coming in, dragging a white buckling.

"But we agreed to survey the area first," Samuel complained with disapproval.

"I've surveyed the surroundings carefully, don't worry. There's no one around. Besides, one has to take the initiative to set the wheels of a true adventure in motion. And the first step is always dangerous and breathtaking."

Suddenly they heard voices. They looked at each other in alarm and listened.

"They were here, I swear, I saw them."

It was the voice of a child, a girl, speaking in Somali.

"Where did you see them? How many were they?"

"There were two boys."

"Are you sure?"

"I'm sure. I swear I'm telling the truth."

Samuel looked at Danny with wide open eyes. Danny stared back in horror. Samuel quickly seized the buckling's neck with his left hand and clutched its mouth tightly with his right hand to prevent it from making a noise. The buckling struggled fiercely but Danny seized its four legs with both hands, forced it to lie down on the ground, and applied both his knees on his stomach to prevent it from moving. The buckling struggled desperately to free itself, but the boys were more desperate and too strong for it.

The voices outside came closer.

"Are you sure you saw two boys?" the adult quizzed her.

"With my own eyes. I swear! They were in the bushes first, for a long time. Then they disappeared from my sight. Then they were there again. I think they came from that direction. Then I decided to run to you and tell you."

Samuel flashed two fingers without lifting his left hand. Danny nodded in agreement. From their retreating voice, the boys guessed that the Somalis were going down the river, towards Dolo. Samuel waited for a moment.

"We must escape! Wait until I give you the signal. Then we must run in the opposite direction as fast as we can. If we're trapped on all sides, we should jump into the river and swim and come out on the other side."

Samuel waited fixing his eyes on Danny. Danny nodded in agreement.

"One, two, three!"

They released the buckling, seized their belongings and went out from their hiding, running with all their might.

"There!" they heard the girl screaming.

The distance between them was about a hundred paces or less.

"Thieves! Thieves!" shouted the adult and gave chase, hurling both stones and a torrent of obscene words at them.

Even though the boys were very tired, they ran for their lives. Fortunately for them, the adult was wearing a *macawis*, a long skirt-like garment, which was not suitable for running freely. Nevertheless, he pulled his skirts up in one hand and pursued them for a kilometer or so before giving up. The boys ran for a long time, taking short breaks in between. They could not be certain that they were safe. At last, having completely exhausted their energy and being saturated in sweat, they stopped and collapsed on the ground, desperately gasping for air and thirsting for water.

Chapter 12

They rested for about ten minutes, then Samuel stood up, put on his shoes, and collected his bag and staff, ready to resume the journey. Danny wanted to complain, but instead stood up reluctantly. He had been feeling guilty for having been stubborn and for having exposed them both to great danger.

"We can cool ourselves down in the river before we set off. You can go first. I'll keep watch," said Samuel coolly, avoiding Danny's eyes.

Danny undressed and went into the river. Samuel kept watch, anxiously fixing his eyes in the direction from which they had come. There was no one following them. When Danny returned, Samuel took his turn in the water but returned quickly. Then they set off and travelled for about another hour without talking to one another.

Around noon the heat became intolerable, the air too stagnant, and they felt very hungry and tired. Yet they travelled onwards, searching for a suitable place to rest. At last, they arrived at a place where the river passed between two gentle hills, and on the hill to their right they saw two dwarf and dusty acacia trees standing alone.

"We will stay there for the rest of the day. We shall resume our journey tomorrow, early in the morning."

Samuel squeezed his hat and jacket into his bag, threw the bag and the staff over the river and then swam across. Afterwards, putting on his jacket, he approached the trees with the intent of inspecting his surroundings.

"This will do for one night," he called out.

Danny also threw his clothes over the river and swam to the other side. Upon reaching the riverbank, he immediately felt safer.

"I'll go fishing," Samuel announced when Danny joined him. "I very much hope that the river contains some fish for us. Otherwise, I don't know how we'll survive the day. If you feel strong enough, you can collect twigs."

Danny threw himself on the ground and closed his eyes. Samuel left, taking his fishing gear with him.

Danny slept until late in the afternoon. As soon as he was awake, he ventured to the other side of the hill to collect twigs. By the time he had returned, towards sundown, Samuel was still not back. Even though the sun was declining, it was not yet dark. A little worried, Danny went down to the river to look for Samuel, but Samuel was not at the river. He searched along the river, both southwards and northwards, but he could not find Samuel. Perplexed and anxious, he stood by the river and waited, desperately longing to see the figure of Samuel emerging from somewhere. Then he heard Samuel calling him, his voice coming from among the trees. He hurried to Samuel.

"Where were you? I was very worried. What's this?"

He stopped and retreated backwards, very disturbed by the sight in front of him. Samuel was holding a dead snake with his staff, a big dark-brown mamba, about two meters long.

"I had no luck today. I couldn't catch a single fish. Then I went up to the hilltop in search of something to eat and this is what I found."

"But it's a snake…" Danny whispered with indignation.

"Don't be afraid, it's dead."

"I can see it's dead! Why did you bring it here?"

"This will be our supper today."

"What?"

"We've no option. We have to roast it and eat it."

Disgusted by the thought, Danny turned his face away and spat on the ground.

"What's left for us if we refuse to eat this snake is starvation. We've consumed all the biscuits and we've no fish left."

"I'd rather die than eat this repugnant creature."

"Well, that's your choice."

"Have you ever eaten a snake before?"

"I haven't."

"How can you be sure it's not poisonous?"

"I'm not sure whether it's poisonous or not, but we can grill it properly."

"Why can't we search for something else? We can search for cactus fruit and wild berries. I'm sure we can find some."

"Believe me there is no wild fruit I haven't already searched for. I couldn't find anything. This place is desolate. I didn't kill the snake thinking we could eat it. But after I'd killed it, the thought struck me. Who knows, maybe someone has taken pity on us?"

"You mean God?"

"Maybe."

"Do you think God cares for us?"

"Don't you think so?"

"I don't know what to think. But if God cares for us, shouldn't he have a better plan for us than this!"

"I'm going ahead with my plan."

"Please yourself. Don't count me in."

"Can you make a fire while I skin the snake?"

Danny arranged the wood to make a fire and Samuel prepared the ground to skin the snake.

"You have gathered a large amount of wood in a short time. You have done a good job," Samuel remarked, not only because he wanted to make peace with him but also because Danny had indeed tried hard to collect a large amount of wood.

Danny was pleased that Samuel wanted to make peace with him, but he still looked at him with great disapproval and reservation. The twigs burnt quickly, the fire illuminating the camp. Samuel brought out his pocket knife and cut the snake's head off. Then he stripped off the skin and removed the gut.

"I bet this is not your first time eating such as disgusting creature. I can see from the way you dress the snake," remarked Danny.

"Believe me, this is my first time. I'm only applying common sense. Even though I've never skinned a snake before, I've helped the prophet skin sheep and goats and the likes on numerous occasions. The procedure should be the same. I'll tell you something. No meat is disgusting if it's fresh and grilled properly. So, my dear friend, I'm going to grill this snake and we both will eat it, because tomorrow a long and tedious journey awaits us."

"I'll never put the meat of this disgusting creature into my mouth."

"Then you'll die of starvation."

"I'd rather die."

"You are not much of an encouragement."

"You're really asking a lot!"

Samuel cut the meat into pieces and, lifting each piece with a stick, started to grill the meat.

"This meat isn't fatty, I can tell from its smell," he observed, looking at Danny mischievously.

"I don't care!"

After he had thoroughly grilled the meat, Samuel studied it closely. Either he had been hiding his true feelings from the start or it suddenly occurred to him what he was about to eat, so that he contorted his face with unconcealed disgust.

"Huh!" Danny released a chuckle. "Look at our open-minded survivor!"

"Oh my, what am I doing!" Samuel moaned and closed his eyes.

Danny laughed heartily even though he himself was feeling miserable from tiredness and starvation.

With his eyes still closed, Samuel took a small bite from the piece and tasted the meat. He took some time to weigh up his reaction and then opened his eyes.

"It's rather tasteless, or rather tastes like a soft rubber, but nothing too disgusting."

"So, go on, let's see how you enjoy your meal!" Danny scoffed good-naturedly.

Samuel took another bite and yet another.

"Really, you should taste it. It's not that bad at all. Although, I admit it's not something I'd have willingly eaten had there been any other option."

Danny declined the offer and watched Samuel expectantly, as if he was waiting for something to happen. But nothing happened and Samuel finished the first piece and started to grill the second piece.

"I'll grill everything tonight and we can take the leftovers with us tomorrow, or else it'll get spoiled."

Danny lay on the ground on his stomach and closed his eyes, listening to the ceaseless gnawing in the pit of his stomach and the throbbing of his entire body. At long last, he opened his eyes and sat up and stared at Samuel. Samuel was eating the second piece without looking at him.

"Oh, damn it, give it here!" he exploded.

He stood up, darted to Samuel, snatched the piece of snake meat from his hand, and took a hefty bite.

"Eat slowly, otherwise you'll be sick."

Danny did not pay attention. Instead, he took multiple bites, chewed very quickly, and swallowed, as it were, without actually tasting the meat he was eating.

"It isn't that bad, is it?"

"I don't care. Are you grilling some more or not?"

They ate about half of the snake that night. As soon as they had finished cooking, Samuel wrapped the rest in some leaves he had cut from the nearby bushes and hung it on one of the trees. Then he made his bed next to the fire and fell asleep instantly. But Danny, despite being very exhausted, was not ready to sleep. His mind was alert, as it was accustomed to being most nights. He sat by the fire, put some twigs onto it, and tried to reflect on how the day had gone by and what the coming days might contain for him and for Samuel.

Now that he felt healthy and strong, he did not mind much going back to Neghelle to lead a normal life. He was confident that he would excel at school. He wanted to be useful for his mother who was almost certainly a widow by now. He had already decided not to tell his mother about his father's affair with Zema. The news would upset her very much. It was better not to talk about it, not to remember it, not to think about it. But his mother would miss Zema terribly, for she had been her friend, her comforter, her helper, and her confidante. He had to fill her place by helping his siblings with school work and his mother with running the household. He desperately wanted to be a good boy. He also wanted to be successful in sport. He had to find a club where he could play football.

"But first we have to reach Neghelle safely," he thought painfully and released a heavy sigh.

"And how about Samuel? What will become of him?" he asked himself anxiously.

He did not know. He did not want to think about Samuel's fate. It was painful to think about Samuel's fate. Danny did not want to depart from Samuel, for he liked, admired, and respected Samuel. Life with him the past few days had been exceptionally peaceful and full of possibilities. No, he did not want to think about Samuel's destiny now.

"We have to live one day at a time," he sighed for the second time. "Besides, I don't know what awaits us tomorrow, the day after tomorrow, and the day after that. It's a vast and uncertain wilderness we're travelling through. I have to live one day at a time."

But he could not help thinking about Samuel's and his own fate.

"What will become of us? Where will we be next week at this time? Will we be alive? Where will we be?"

Chapter 13

He sat for a long time thinking about many things but without being able to think purposefully and clearly. At the same time, he felt weary and powerless and, for some reason, sad. He forgot that he had been happy only the day before. Throwing the last handful of remaining twigs into the fire, he lay down on his back on his father's jacket next to Samuel, wishing he could sleep.

Suddenly, he heard a rustling noise and became attentive. He quickly turned his head left and right unable to determine from where the noise had come. It could not be the wind swishing through the tree branches, he thought swiftly. It was a windless evening. The noise became louder and he stood up quickly in alarm. Not very far away he could see in the dim light the figures of men closing in on them from all directions.

"Wake up Samuel, we're surrounded!" he screamed on top of his voice.

The men rushed towards him and seized him. One of them drew a sharp knife and put it to his throat and told Danny to keep quiet. He was speaking in Somali. Two men swiftly tied his hands behind his back. Samuel, too, came under assault and his hands were tied behind his back. The men gathered up all of their belongings, extinguished the fire with dust, and led them forcefully towards the river.

"They belong to the infidels," Danny heard one of them speaking in Somali.

"Where can the adults be? What can they be seeking here?" asked another, apparently believing that they were travelling with adults.

When they reached the river, they saw the shadows of men on the other side waiting for their comrades and beaming flashlights in their direction. These men threw a long, sturdy rope over the river to their comrades and the rope was suspended by two men on each side. Three of their abductors removed their macawis and wore them like scarves around their necks and crossed the river walking, supporting themselves by taking hold of the rope. Two of them crossed the river carrying Samuel and Danny on their shoulders. Finally, the two men holding the rope released it and crossed the river swimming, holding their *macawis*, shirt, and sticks, as well as the items they confiscated from the boys in their hands.

Once on the other side, they marched westwards. The abductors were seven men altogether.

"We haven't done you any harm, please let us go," Samuel begged them in Amharic. When they heard him speak Amharic they were furious. One of them hurled obscenities at Samuel and slapped him in the face.

"Keep quiet!" he thundered.

"He's telling you to keep quiet," Danny translated in whisper.

He too received a heavy slap in the face, so that his eyes were temporarily blinded.

"We mustn't take them to the village. We should find out what they're up to and finish them here if we must," suggested one of them.

"They should first lead us to the accursed soldier," answered another.

"They want to kill us, should I tell them that I can speak their language?" Danny risked retribution and whispered to Samuel.

There was no immediate retribution. Instead, one of the men, the one with the sharp knife, sternly ordered him to be quiet and hurled obscenities at him once again.

"If you tell them, they may take us for spies. Just wait a little, until we know what they're up to," Samuel ventured to add in a whisper after a moment's deliberation. This time he was struck in the head with a stick and fell on the ground.

"Get up on your feet, you swine!" The man with the knife shouted and pulled him back to his feet.

"Calm down," came an order from a tall and lean man who appeared to be the leader of the group.

"He should learn to obey," retorted the man and hurled obscenities.

"Shouldn't we stay here and wait until morning?" inquired one of them.

"We've waited long enough," replied the man with the knife. "There was no one in the vicinity. Whoever has sent them here on a mission is either deliberately hiding or not here."

"We are taking a great risk in taking them to the village," warned another man.

"We have the right to find out what they are up to. We have the right to defend our people and our properties."

"We should stay here until daybreak and see who comes to rescue them."

"That would be a waste of time. We should interrogate them now and find out what they're up to."

There arose a heated debate between the men. Some of them were afraid that soldiers would be dispatched to search for the boys, which might lead to the torture and rape of women and girls. This group was in favor of interrogating the boys on the way, and, if need be, by torturing them. The others were of the opinion that since the country was at war and short of soldiers, it could not afford to send soldiers. Moreover, by delaying the interrogation, they were hoping to find out who would come to rescue the boys. This group was in favor of taking time to interrogate the boys. All of them, however, believed that the boys had been sent on a mission, either to spy on the nomads or to test their loyalty. From their conversation Danny determined that the men had been tracking them for a long time that day.

After they had travelled for about fifteen minutes or so, the calm man ordered his men to blindfold the boys.

"Why should we bother, it's dark already. They can't distinguish anything," encountered the man with the knife.

"Still, we should blindfold them."

"Are we intending to release them?"

"This cannot be determined now."

"We should use them as hostages and bargain with the infidels or demand a ransom." Another man suggested.

"We should make them our slaves," suggested another.

"The infidels will find out if we keep slaves in our midst," remarked the man with the knife.

After they had blindfolded Samuel and Danny, the abductors interrupted their journey briefly, apparently, to smoke. Then they resumed with their journey and travelled, much of the time in silence. Danny stumbled and fell three times and each time he was viciously pulled up to his feet. On the fourth occasion, however, the hot-headed man accused him of doing this deliberately and struck him on the head with his stick. They travelled up and down on irregular and dusty paths and finally arrived at a place where they decided to sojourn. They sent for a certain Usman Ali to come and receive them.

Presently, the men lit cigarettes and talked calmly about the casualties the Ethiopian soldiers had sustained and the vast expanse of land the Somali soldiers had conquered in the east in such a short time. Some of the men made their own estimation of how long the war would go on. Some of them said it would take a further three months, some of them said six months, and some of them said not more than an extra month. But all of them were firmly convinced that the war would be concluded by Somalia vanquishing Ethiopia and claiming the entire Ogaden region for itself. From their talk Danny was unable to determine whether they were sympathetic to their kin on the other side of the border. Most of them seemed rather more concerned with the outrageous rise in the price of crops and sugar and put the blame on the war.

Usman Ali arrived with the messenger and exchanged greetings with the abductors. The leader explained where and in what condition they had found the boys.

"Did you find out why they are here?"

The calm man answered in the negative. From the way the men talked to Usman Ali and from his authoritative voice, Samuel and Danny suspected that he was an important man. The abductors did not seem to have any connection with the man and his daughter whom the boys had encountered earlier.

Another round of disputes ensued because the men could not agree on what to do with the boys. Usman Ali was of the opinion that they would not gain anything in keeping them in the village, except trouble. He explained that none of the surrounding villages would be willing to hide the boys, should they decide to keep them somewhere else. He suggested releasing them immediately and mind their own business or "getting rid of them".

The calm man argued that should the war be extended, the villagers would be in a difficult position to purchase crops and sugars from the surrounding towns.

"It's expedient to keep the boys alive and to use them as hostages."

But many voices vehemently opposed his idea because they were afraid of being discovered by the "infidel soldiers" or their informants.

"Suppose we are being watched, being spied on?" Usman Ali asked the calm man.

"But nobody has come to rescue them. It's very likely that they're alone on a mission."

"What do you think they're doing here on their own?"

"We should interrogate them tomorrow morning and find out."

"Suppose the boys were given up as sacrifices?"

"Sacrifices? To gain what?"

"I don't know. Suppose the infidels want to test our loyalty?"

"With the lives of their own children?"

"They might have kidnapped them. The boys were certainly on their way from Dolo. What soldier permits his child to live in Dolo? No, these are street boys the soldiers can easily dispose of without any regret."

"In that case, killing them will do us no good. Whoever has sent them will eventually find out what we've done to them."

"So what if they find out?" Usman Ali shouted angrily. "No matter what we do, the infidels will always think we're traitors. We've been subject to humiliation on a number of occasions. We must give them a lesson and show them that we're proud and independent people, capable of and ready to defend our honor."

"If we keep them alive for a couple of days, we shall find out who is behind them and what they're seeking to gain." The argument continued for some time but, at last, they agreed to delay their decision until morning. It had not occurred to them that one of the boys could speak their language or, perhaps, they did not care.

Having thus settled their dispute for the night, they brought them into a hut which was full of goats and donkeys. They tied them up back to back on a short wooden pole embedded in the ground in the middle of the room and left them there with their eyes still blindfolded.

Chapter 14

As soon as the men had left, Danny told Samuel in a whisper the substance of their abductor's disputes.

"They've agreed to interrogate us tomorrow. I must speak to them in their language. I must explain everything."

"Since they've decided to interrogate us," whispered back Samuel, "there must be at least one of them who knows Amharic. But, if that's the case, then they've understood what we've been saying the whole time! Apparently, none of them could speak Amharic until now."

"Maybe if I tell them that my mother is a Somali, they may change their minds about us."

"Perhaps, about you. Perhaps not."

"What should we do?"

"We must act tonight."

"In our condition? What can we do?"

"I don't know yet."

"These people want to kill us, it's no joke. My life just started to get interesting and then comes this!"

"We mustn't tell them that you speak their language. They'll think that we've already heard more than enough to be released. Moreover, they'll debate everything in our absence tomorrow. In which case, we'll have no way finding out their plan."

"Who do you think is the 'accursed soldier'?"

"Obviously a soldier who's insulted them."

"They were talking about the raping of women and girls."

"If indeed a soldier has done such a horrible thing to their people, our lives are in great danger."

"I told you so."

"If that's the case, they'll definitely harm us."

"What should we do?"

"I'm at a loss."

"I must speak to them."

"If you do, there's a possibility that they may not harm you. But it'll not change my situation. For you'll have to tell them how we met. I'm almost certain that they will not believe my account. Neither should you forget the fact that you're a great risk to them. They may not harm you, but they may also not release you. You already know too much."

"You said you've travelled a lot with the prophet. Has anyone ever tried to harm you?"

"No one's ever tried to harm us."

"I've heard my father and the other soldiers talking about the danger of travelling in the wilderness."

"Wherever we travelled, we never had any trouble. Perhaps this was because there was peace at the time."

"How often did you travel in this region with the prophet?"

"This is the second time I've travelled in the wilderness."

"Was the prophet with you when you travelled the first time?"

"No."

"Why not?"

"The first time I travelled in this region was when I came to Dolo, searching for the prophet. The prophet must have travelled alone."

"You mean you and the prophet have never travelled in this region together?"

"No, we have never travelled in this region together."

"But you said your prophet travelled extensively and you travelled with him a lot."

"Yes, but in different regions."

"You told me on the first day when we met on the hill that you knew your way around in this region."

"I've brought you this far, haven't I?"
"That wasn't my question, Samuel."
"We're wasting precious time arguing unnecessarily."
"How could you claim that you knew your way around when you had travelled only once in this region?"
"Travelling once is sufficient to know one's way around."
"You've been lying to me."
"Now you're being disrespectful."
"What shall we do now?"
"We should try to escape, that's what we must do. Can you reach the knots in the ropes around my wrists and untie them?"
"You two keep quiet!" thundered a shrieking voice from another room.

So, there was someone in the other room assigned to keep watch over them. Danny tried to reach the knots to free Samuel's wrists, but he could not. Samuel tried to push his wrists up, but their hands were tied tightly together, so that Danny released a stifled scream of pain. Suddenly, they heard the sound of someone striking a match and then walking into the room. From the smell of gas and a faint glow of light, they guessed that the man was holding a gas lantern in his hand.

The man came close to them and examined their fetters. When he ascertained that everything was in place, he put a sharp knife on Samuel's neck and screamed in his ear.

"Keep quiet or I'll slit your throat for you."

Samuel shuddered from the cold touch of the knife.

The man left and silence ensued. Danny felt his brain throbbing ceaselessly from lack of sleep. As if the senses of sight, hearing, and smell had complimentary properties, now his sense of smell became sharper than ever. He felt very sick from the stench of dung. However hard he tried to concentrate and think about their fate, his mind was unable to dwell on the subject. Mundane and irrelevant thoughts and images kept interfering with each other and exacerbated his sickness. After a desperate struggle, he finally threw up and made his own contribution to the repulsive smell.

"Try to breathe with your mouth and not with your nose," Samuel whispered.

Eventually, Danny dozed off into an uneasy sleep and dreamt about horrible things happening to them. Samuel, on the other hand, could not sleep and stayed awake until daybreak. Very early in the morning, he heard the footsteps of men coming into the room.

"Wake up Danny, they've come to take us," Samuel whispered and nudged him.

"I am awake," Danny replied.

The men untied them from the pole but left their hands tied. One of them showered obscenities on Danny when he saw what he had done last night. They hauled them to their feet and led them out, still blindfolded. They walked on foot for about ten minutes and arrived at a place surrounded by big red rocks and densely planted euphorbia trees. There they made them sit on the rocks and removed their blindfolds. The boys were greatly relieved at being able to see once again.

In front of them were five men sitting on clean and colorful reed mats, with their legs crossed, forming a half-circle. All of them were wearing *macawis* with colorful shirts on top and *koofiyad* on their heads. In the middle, a conspicuously tall and slender old man was sitting, most probably the eldest amongst them. Two big silver colored teapots and a plate filled with freshly baked biscuits were placed in the middle and a small tea glass filled with milk tea was standing in front of each man. Some of the men were carrying rifles, M1 Garand, on their left sides. Two of the four men who had brought them from the hut remained standing next to them, but the other two joined the men who were sitting.

The men studied the boys with dispassionate, penetrating eyes. At last, the man in the middle, Usman Ali (they recognized him from his voice), addressed them in Somali. "Who are you boys and what are you doing in this area?" Danny was just about to reply in Somali when a man sitting next to Usman Ali began to translate.

"The old man tells 'what you do'?"

"My name is Samuel," Samuel responded without waiting for Danny, "and this is my little brother Danny. We were coming from Dolo and going to Neghelle. We were fleeing from the war in Dolo."

The man translated Samuel's statement correctly. Apparently, his listening comprehension was better than his speaking skills. Danny was surprised by Samuel's unexpected lie but preferred to keep quiet.

"You two," the translator tapped his own face with his right index finger twice and waved the same finger left and right to suggest that Samuel and Danny did not look alike. Then he added: "You are red, he is black."

"This is because our mothers are different. We have the same father."

"What were you two doing in Dolo?" asked Usman Ali.

"The old man asks…"

This time the translator spent some time searching for the right words and looked to his left and to his right in case someone was able to assist him. When no help was forthcoming, he waived his hands as a sign of helplessness and sipped from his tea glass.

"The old man asks," he then continued, "'what work Dolo'?"

Samuel involuntarily looked at Danny, to ascertain that the man had translated correctly. Danny quickly turned his face away not to give themselves away.

"We went to Dolo to search for work," Samuel replied.

"They were working in Dolo," translated the man.

"Where are your parents and what are you doing here alone?"

"The old man tells, the old man speaks, … the old man asks, 'where father, where mother'?"

"We don't know where our parents are."

"They have no parents," he translated.

"What were you doing in this region alone?"

"The old man tells," he indicated with his index finger once at Danny and once at Samuel and then at the ground, "'do here?'"

"We were running away from the war. We were afraid of being trapped in the war. We couldn't find a truck to take us to Neghelle. Therefore, we decided to travel on foot, following the river," Samuel explained.

"He said they were trapped in the war, but they managed to escape. They were afraid. Then while travelling to Neghelle on a truck, the truck sank in the river. All the people except the boys sank and perished."

"But the road is far away from the river, how can it sink in the river?" Usman Ali frowned.

"The old man says you lie. The road far from the river." Samuel was puzzled but did not want to look at Danny.

"We travelled on foot along the river because there was no truck."

Either he was confused or defiant, the man refused to translate.

"How many people sank and died in the river?" Usman Ali wished to know.

"How many...," once again the man searched for the right word, but when he could not find any, showed with his index finger the sign of slitting a throat, and added, "in the river?"

This time Samuel glanced at Danny in confusion. Danny stepped in quickly.

"No truck sank in the river," he explained in Amharic. "No one died in the river. We travelled on foot. We travelled from Dolo. We travelled on foot, because there was no truck to take us to Neghelle."

In his turn, the translator looked at Danny and then at Samuel in confusion and tried to comprehend Danny's reply. Finally, he turned to Usman Ali.

"The two contradict one another. The red said all were dead, but the black said all were alive, only the truck sank. The boys are lying."

"Slap him in the face," Usman Ali ordered the man standing next to Samuel.

Almost instantly Samuel recoiled from the impact of the hefty strike to his face. His eyes were blinded and his mouth was filled with fresh blood.

"Tell the truth," he heard the translator demanding.

'If this confusion continues,' Danny thought, 'they'll certainly kill us.'

Feeling guilty for the slap Samuel had received, he repeated his last answer in Somali. When they heard him speak fluent Somali, they stared at one another, dumbfounded.

"Why didn't you tell us that you could speak our tongue?" Usman Ali asked him, this time more calmly.

"I was afraid."

"Afraid of what?"

"Afraid of being taken for a spy or an informer."

"Why should we take you for a spy or an informer?"

"I don't know."

"Are you a Muslim?"

Danny did not answer immediately.

"Well?"

"I am not, sir, but my mother is a Muslim."

"Why aren't you a Muslim?"

"I don't know why. I grew up in a mixed family."

"Does your brother speak our language?"

"He doesn't."

"Why is that?"

"We belong to different mothers. My mother is a Somali but his is from Middle Land."

"Is it true that neither of you knows where your parents are?"

"I know where my mother is but Samuel doesn't."

"How is that?"

"Samuel was adopted by a priest when he was a child. Now he doesn't know where his mother or the priest is."

"And where is your mother?"

"My mother lives in Neghelle. I ran away from her because she was a poor woman."

"And your father?"

"We don't know where my, our, father is. He left us when we were still children."

"This one seems to be speaking the truth." Usman Ali concluded. Then he turned his attention to Samuel.

"Tell me, young man, why did you lie to us?"

"The old man tells," the translator began, but Usman Ali put out his left hand and interrupted him.

"Let his brother translate for him."

"I told him that my mother is still alive, but that you don't know where your mother is. Now he wants to know why you lied to him," Danny quickly addressed Samuel, avoiding his eyes.

"Which lie does he refer to?"

"I'm not sure. Perhaps, he was referring to our not knowing where our parents are."

"If you mean, sir, about the whereabouts of our parents, I was referring to my mother. I apologize, I haven't made that clear," replied Samuel.

Danny translated.

"What was your father's profession, what did he do for a living?" Usman Ali addressed Danny this time.

"My, our, father was…"

Danny did not wish to reveal the truth about his father thinking that their interrogators were hostile to soldiers. But he was worked up trying to give a consistent account, so that he could not instantly think of a suitable job for his father.

'If they decide to interrogate us separately," he thought swiftly, "we're toast.'

"Our father used to work as a guard for a military family in Neghelle," he replied, remembering their own guard at home. Then he added, "but he left us a long time ago. I don't know what he does now or whether he's still alive." The last statement was hard for him to finish, because it contained some truth.

"What sort of work did you do in Dolo?"

"You mean, I?"

"I mean both of you."

"We did whatever work we could find. We sold cigarettes, sugarcane, salvage, biscuits, and the likes. We polished shoes and washed clothes for the soldiers, ran errands to merchant women; all sorts of jobs, sir."

"These are the sort of children one would use as informants and spies. They can go anywhere and carry out all sorts of errands and no one misses them if they disappear or are dead," commented the man who had drawn his knife yesterday.

"Your father was a military officer, wasn't he?" the calm man asked Danny.

"No, he wasn't."

"The jacket we confiscated from you yesterday, it's an officer's jacket. Wasn't it your father's jacket? We've found some documents in it."

Danny was stunned. Could it be possible that he had overlooked documents in his father's jacket all this time?

"The jacket was a gift from an officer for whom I used to polish shoes and ran errands."

"You two are proper swindlers, aren't you?" the calm man stared at Danny with a pair of piercing eyes, but without lifting his voice.

"I swear by all the holy angels; I'm telling the truth!" Danny whined desperately.

"Or, perhaps the jacket was stolen?"

"No, sir, I didn't steal it. It was a gift. There was a time when I was very ill and coughing terribly all day long. The officer had pity on me and gave me his jacket."

The men in the middle exchanged some words in low voices.

"We have given you a chance to tell us the truth," Usman Ali finally addressed the boys, "but you haven't used your chance wisely. Therefore, we have decided to teach you lesson."

The man spoke with a toneless voice, his small, ghostly eyes slowly shifting from side to side to study their reaction separately. The boys involuntarily noticed that his front teeth were all rotten and his canine teeth on both sides were replaced by gold teeth.

"You'll be committing a crime if you torture us," Samuel addressed Usman Ali and asked Danny to translate for him. Danny translated.

"You will gain nothing by torturing us, because we have done you no wrong. We ran away from Dolo in order to save our lives. No one sent us here. We work for no one. Your men seized us while we were resting, exhausted from a long and tedious journey. We haven't stolen a goat from your flock nor eaten from your field. I'm begging you to let us go in peace."

"This one is skillful in making a speech," said the man with the knife, meaning Samuel. "The infidels have trained him very well. We have to make him sing."

Presently, Usman Ali stretched out his hand to pick up some biscuits from the plate in front of him and gave his final order.

"Blindfold them and take them away. Place them separately."

Chapter 15

The boys were blindfolded and the same strong hands which had hustled them in the morning into the assembly now clutched them under their armpits and brought them to their feet and hustled them back to the hut where they had spent the previous night. But when they had walked about two hundred paces, they suddenly heard a calm, measured voice from behind.

"Don't move one step forward or I'll blow your heads off!"

It was the voice of a male speaking in accented Somali, clearly revealing that he was not a Somali. The men obeyed.

"Untie the boys and remove the blindfolds from their eyes."

No one moved. Danny, barely comprehending what was just unfolding, repeated the order with feverish excitement. The men were stunned by the sudden turn of events, so that they did not react to the demands of the stranger immediately.

When they looked back, they could see an armed soldier standing behind them, approximately five or six meters away, aiming an M14 rifle at them. He was wearing a light-green protective combat helmet, desert military camouflage attire, and a pair of heavy military boots. On his back he was carrying a heavy American military backpack. He was in his mid-forties, dark-skinned, tall, muscular, and broad-shouldered.

"Untie the boys now, hurry up, or I'll blow your heads off."

One of the men hurried to untie the boys whereas the others remained standing, not daring to make a movement. But the man's hands were visibly shaking and he was unable to untie the boys. Moments later two of them came to his aid and untied the boys as a fourth removed their blindfolds. The boys had been hustled along by four men. Only one of them was armed.

"Can either of you boys handle a rifle?" the soldier asked in Amharic.

"I can," Danny hurried to answer.

"Very well. Take the gun from him and check if it is loaded."

The man refused to surrender his rifle but his comrades urged him to give it up, whereupon he reluctantly handed it over to Danny. Danny checked the rifle and determined that it was loaded.

"Do you know how to eject the cartridge from the firing chamber?"

"Yes, sir!"

"Good. Eject the bullet and remove the clip. Then count all the bullets. Check very carefully," the soldier ordered him without taking his eyes off the men.

Danny did as he was told.

"There are eight bullets."

"Very well. Now reinsert the clip. The rifle should load automatically when you remove your thumb from the clip. Be careful with the clip."

"I know how to load an M1 rifle, sir," Danny announced and loaded the gun immaculately.

"Now you boys come to me."

When Samuel and Danny had joined the soldier, he ordered the men to stand side by side and to put their hands on their heads. Then he ordered them to turn back and go slowly forwards to the assembly.

"The men in the assembly are armed with rifles," Danny warned the soldier.

"Don't worry, I know these cowards very well."

The four men, all of them in their early twenties, moved forwards with measured steps and the soldier and the boys followed them from behind, the soldier and Danny aiming their rifles at them. Because of the surrounding euphorbia trees the men in the assembly learned of what was going on only when it was too late. All of them stood up in alarm at the sight of the soldier, those who kept rifles on their side reaching for their rifles instinctively. But before they could take up their rifles the soldier yelled at them and ordered them to refrain.

"What's it you want, soldier? You promised not to trouble us again," Usman Ali addressed the soldier with an apparent resignation.

"The old man tells," began the translator.

"Oh, not you again! Keep quiet!" the soldier barked at him.

Meanwhile, the soldier counted the men and seemed to be satisfied with the outcome. Apparently, he knew how many men dwelt in that village. Then, turning to Danny he ordered him to translate for him.

"Usman Ali, you treacherous old snake! What were you going to do with these two unarmed and harmless boys who happened to pass your village by?"
Danny dropped the "treacherous old snake" part and translated the rest.
"My dear sir, some of our men found these two boys in suspicious circumstances yesterday evening and brought them here. We wanted to find out what they were doing. You must understand, honorable sir, that this is a time of war. It is our duty to know what is going on in and around our village."
"They brought us here forcefully. They beat us, fettered us, and kept us in a stinking stall. Even now, sir, they were taking us to the village in order to torture us. They accused us of being informants to the infidel soldiers," Danny confronted Usman Ali furiously.
Usman Ali, somehow realizing that the boy was speaking ill of him, defended his actions.
"Please don't take heed to everything the boys say, honorable soldier. They gave us contradictory accounts of their identities and the purpose of their presence in our region. It was our duty to establish the truth."
"I happened to have cavesdropped during your interrogation," the soldier told him.

"Very well, sir. It's my sincere hope that you understand our dilemma. We're living in very difficult times."

"You'll have to give account to those soldiers whom you've insulted, you stinking old man. Your repeated show of contempt towards the soldiers who protect you and your property is common knowledge. You're ungrateful. In your heart you think that the war will drag on endlessly and that no one has time to question your distempered unruliness. Well, you're mistaken. Prepare yourself for a visit one of these days. As if that isn't enough, you treat these defenseless boys shamelessly."

Danny translated, almost word for word, breathlessly.

"Calm down my dear sir. We shall explain everything to your complete satisfaction. We're not unruly as you think. We're rather law-abiding inhabitants who are only being cautious."

"Enough of your empty words. Now I'll not ask you to give up your rifles, but I'll ask you to empty them and to give me the bullets."

Upon hearing the translation, Usman Ali showed great defiance.

"This will be done over my dead body, my dear soldier. If you confiscate the bullets, we will not have anything with which to defend our village. This is unacceptable. Neither of my men will accept this," he said coldly.

The men with rifles also looked at the soldier with palpable defiance.

"Look," Usman Ali added calmly, "this will not be necessary. We have permission from the government to arm ourselves. It's not only our village we defend, but also our country. You must remember, respected soldier, that my people love and are loyal to this country, but your actions, sir, test our patience to the limit."

"I don't care for your empty words and I don't have patience for insubordination. Either you do it now or I shall blow off the heads of these men!"

Danny translated in frenzy once again. For some reason he was agitated and desirous to witness some drama and bloodshed. None of the men made any sign of submission. It was clear from the expression of their faces and their posture that they were ready to fight.

"I'll make you an offer," the soldier spoke firmly, after a brief deliberation, "but if you decline, shame be upon you. You'll empty the chambers and remove the clips and give them to me. We shall leave your village peacefully, but you can send two of your men with us. As soon as we've reached a safe place, I shall hand over the bullets to your men. I'll not be asking you this time to send me away with food supplies."

Usman Ali listened to the translation carefully and looked at the men to his right and to his left. The men still looked defiant but he seemed to have made up his mind.

"Submit," he told the three men who were in possession of rifles.

He beckoned one of the young men and ordered him to empty the rifles. The man collected the clips in a piece of cloth and handed them over to the soldier.

"I take you at your word, respected soldier," Usman Ali said, his entire body language revealing his great vexation. "We shall take these two men with us. Make sure that none of your men follows us."

"The rifle, sir, you must return the rifle."

"Remove the clip and the bullet in the chamber and give it back to him," the soldier ordered Danny. Danny did as he was told.

They left the assembly cautiously, the two men leading the way. But before they left the village, Samuel begged the soldier to stop for a moment.

"What for?" the soldier snapped at him.

"I can't go without my belongings, sir, which these people confiscated from me yesterday. I can't survive in the wilderness without them. Please order one of these men to collect all my belongings."

"I can't do that; these people are dangerous. We must leave this place at once!" the soldier whispered emphatically.

"Sir, I can't go without my belongings. Please ask them to return them to me."

The soldier looked cross, but he saw Samuel's desperate look.

"What belongings?"

"A jacket, sir. It was a gift from my old man, whom I've served faithfully for many years. They have also taken my staff, my fishing gear, and some matches. Without them it's impossible for me to survive in the wilderness."

The soldier turned to Danny.

"Have they also taken property from you?"

"My father's jacket."

The soldier called one of the men and ordered him to collect their belongings.

"You will return in five minutes or else you'll never see your friend alive ever again."

The man hurried to the village to collect their belongings. Samuel turned to Danny and pleaded with him to shout after the man not to forget his staff.

"They have no use for it, but I can't live without it."

Danny shouted after the man as Samuel asked him, but he could not be certain that the man had heard him.

"If this man fails to return in five minutes, we shall go without him," retorted the soldier.

But the man came back running, with all their belongings in his hands. Before he came nearer, however, the soldier ordered him to stop and empty the bag, to turn the jackets inside out, and to leave everything on the ground. When he was finished, the soldier ordered him to join his comrade.

"Go and collect them," the soldier ordered Samuel.

In the meantime, Usman Ali and his men were standing behind them at an appreciable distance, watching. Their women and girls along with several naked children, too, were watching them fearfully, standing in front of their squalid huts.

Finally, the soldier ordered the two men to lead onwards, towards the Ganale River. They left the village and joined a dusty footpath, apparently leading to the river. On the way, the soldier asked the boys who they were and what they were doing in the wilderness alone.

"Now, whoever has sent you here on a mission must have been ill-advised or extremely careless. This place is very dangerous even for a veteran soldier let alone for naive children like yourselves. Besides, you aren't even armed. Even if you were armed, they would have easily overpowered you. The army's intelligence department may very well be understaffed, but that doesn't mean it should recklessly throw children into the oven." The soldier turned to Danny. "By now you must have realized that speaking their language isn't enough to win these people's confidence."

Samuel told him their story, but omitting the fact that Danny's father was a military doctor.

"You are not siblings?"

"No, sir, we are not."

"Why did you lie to Usman Ali?"

"Because we were afraid of them."

"Why were you afraid of them?"

"Because we thought that if they knew that Danny's father was a soldier, they'd mistreat us."

Nevertheless, the soldier was unconvinced.

"You can speak in confidence. If you must conceal some specifics, you can at least tell me whom you do work for. Is it for Colonel Tadesse or Captain Alexander? I can't take you into my protection unless I know something about you."

"But I told you the truth, sir. We're on our own. There's no secret mission."

"You couldn't have come to Dolo in search of a prophet! Who's ever heard of a prophet? You travel with a fishing gear, a box of matches, and a knife, like an experienced traveler. You, too," he turned to Danny, "could have not come to Dolo searching for your father. You two are proper swindlers, the old man was right in this regard."

"But we're telling you the truth," Samuel insisted. "You don't take us for spies, do you, sir?"

"I don't know what to take you for! You may be the devil's messengers for all I care. You two have no idea how you messed up my mission! Move quickly you worthless nomads or I'll blow your heads off for you." He snapped at the men in front of them.

"I'm not responsible for you, do you understand? You're on your own. I'll bring you as far as I can and then return to my own business. You, too, will mind your own business. I don't give a damn if you are informants or some commonplace thieves or two irresponsible idiots. I've no obligation whatsoever to protect or keep you."

"It's all right, sir, we can manage by ourselves. We appreciate your help," said Samuel.

"You understand very little of the danger you're in, young man," the soldier scolded him. "Whoever has sent you here didn't care whether you return alive or not. You're his responsibility and not mine."

Nothing was said thereafter for a long time. When he saw the river from afar, the soldier let the men return to their village with all their bullets as he had promised. At the river they rested and he gave the boys canned food to eat. The boys wanted to ask him about the war, but they were afraid of him. He still looked irascible and displeased with them.

"How are you going to go to Neghelle or to any place for that matter where you will be safe? I won't be able to accompany you, because I'm on an important mission. Between here and Neghelle, there are countless hungry beasts desperately waiting to devour flesh and bones."

"We shall be careful, sir," Samuel tried to reassure him for the second time.

At last Danny ventured to raise a question.

"How's the war going on, sir?"

"We're in the middle of it. The enemy have managed to advance swiftly in the east. Sadly, they have already conquered several key cities. But in the south, our soldiers are warding them off."

"Have there been many casualties?"

"Yes, indeed. On both sides. It's a barbaric war."

Danny paused for a while, trying to control himself, before he put in his next question.

"Do you know how many people died in the bomb attack?"

"Which bomb attack are you referring to?" the soldier asked him suspiciously.

"I mean at the medical facility in Dolo."

"Why should it interest you?"

"Because I saw the bombs falling."

"Are you working for the enemy?" the soldier asked Danny suddenly the possibility dawned on him. But the boy's face turned scarlet with indignation, so much so that the soldier did not need to pursue the question any further.

"We lost fifty-two people."

Danny felt a sharp pain shooting through the middle of his heart.

"Do you think we'll retake our cities in the east?"

"We shall fight to the last drop of our blood. This is the spirit we've inherited from our forefathers. Now coming back to you. You must remember that Usman Ali and his men won't give up on you easily. They'll pursue you, send messengers to the villages ahead of you, and try to capture you. They'll not rest until they've learned what you were up to. They always feel as though they are being spied on and want to know why. They may think you have some answer to offer. You must make haste wherever you want to go."

"Thank you, sir, for your advice. We shall be very careful," Samuel reassured the soldier.

"You have very little idea about being very careful, even though from the look of you, you're rather a clever boy."

Then turning to Danny, the soldier addressed him.

"You seem to be a reasonable and brave young man. Why didn't you go to the camp and seek protection there in the first place, instead of running away into the wilderness?"

"We thought the enemy would invade the camp instantly and set it on fire. We decided to run into the wilderness before the main road was cut off."

"Assuming your story has one ounce of truth to it, I still think that you've been unwise in coming to the wilderness."

"Perhaps, you are right, sir. Our decision was made on the spur of the moment. We were very afraid of the war breaking at any moment," Danny consented.

"I'll stay with you until sundown, then I'll get back to my business when it gets dark."

"That's very kind of you, sir. Thank you again for saving our lives."

As soon as they sat down to rest, the boys were overpowered by the need to sleep. The soldier noticed their condition and had pity on them.

"All right, go on, take a nap. I'll keep watch."

Chapter 16

Danny woke up from a deep sleep with a headache and difficulty in opening his eyes. When at last he managed to open them, he saw Samuel lying beside him on his jacket, still fast asleep. It was a windless late-afternoon and the air was still stifling. He got up on his feet with some difficulty and looked around for the soldier, but he was nowhere to be seen. None of his belongings were there. He shook Samuel gently on his shoulder and told him to wake up.

"It's getting late Samuel; we have to leave now."

Samuel too woke up with difficulty but remained immobile, blankly gazing at the dusty ground with half-closed eyes.

"Has the soldier gone already?" he asked at long last.

"It looks like it. It's strange, though, he has left without saying goodbye."

"When did you get up?"

"A short while ago?"

"Has he already left by then?"

"He wasn't there when I woke up."

"I can't imagine him leaving us without saying goodbye. Perhaps, he's gone fishing?"

"Wouldn't he have left his rucksack here?"

"A soldier never leaves his belongings behind. You should know this better than I. I'm almost certain he's somewhere here."

"What shall we do?"

"Speaking of fishing, I'm dying of starvation," bemoaned Samuel still fixing his eyes on the ground.

"We haven't eaten anything since we ate that disgusting snake yesterday evening, and that's nearly twenty-four hours ago."

"But the soldier gave us the canned food, have you forgotten?"

"Oh, yes, the canned food! Now I remember. I'm starving."

"Me too."

"Anyway, you should be thankful; the disgusting snake saved your life."

"I'd give anything right now to have another piece of snake meat."

Samuel dragged his body into a sitting position, pulled his knees towards his body and tightly embraced them with his arms.

"I've no strength left to take a single step tonight," he bemoaned once again.

"But we're not safe here, Samuel. If Usman Ali's men have decided to pursue us, they'll capture us here tonight."

"I know, I know. But I've no strength left. I'm a human being after all."

"Come on, Samuel. Up to now you've been the strongest of us both. Don't give up. Get up to your feet!"

"Maybe we should give up on following the river and travel eastwards. Otherwise, Usman Ali's men will surely catch up with us if we continue to follow the river."

"But if we abandon the river, it'll be the end of us; we shall die of thirst and hunger."

"What bad luck that we stumbled upon the Somalis."

"But that was inevitable, wasn't it? The wilderness is their dwelling place."

"How about if we cross the river and move a little away from it and spend the night there? I can't move today and I've no strength left for fishing."

Danny sat next to Samuel feeling helpless and abandoned. Neither did he have sufficient strength left to do anything other than rest. But the prospect of being captured by the men they had left behind weighed very heavily on him. While the sun slowly made its exit, the boys sat side by side in silence and Samuel began to slumber gradually. Danny struggled to stay awake, but having nothing to do, he, too, lay down on the ground and fell asleep.

But his sleep was interrupted when a firm hand shook him on his shoulder. He started in panic and opened his eyes. It was the soldier.

"It's time to get up and make a fire."

He had already piled up twigs and a freshly killed animal was lying on the ground next to the twigs. At first Danny thought it was a goat but it was not.

"What's that?" he asked the soldier, pointing at the animal, and not trusting his eyes.

"How should I know?" the soldier rebuffed him, searching for something in his backpack.

"Where did you get it?" Danny asked him foolishly, suddenly invaded by an explosive joy at the prospect of having something to eat.

"I sought for a kill for more than two hours and was about to give up when I suddenly saw the lonesome creature in front of its cave."

"How did you manage to gather so many twigs at the same time?"

"This is what you learn to do when you become a soldier."

"Samuel, get up!" Danny screamed with excitement. "We're saved! We've something to eat. The soldier hasn't abandoned us. Get up."

But Samuel refused to be bothered.

Meanwhile, the soldier prepared the animal for skinning.

"I need your help," he told Danny. "Hold the right legs tight, one with each hand."

With his combat knife he made cuts around the bends of each leg and along the interiors of the legs. Then he cut the skin in a straight line from the throat down to the genital area and started to skillfully detach the skin from the animal's body by gently applying force sometimes with his fist and sometimes with the bolster of his knife, but rarely with the blade of the knife. The animal had been killed with a single bullet to its flank.

"We've never seen a single animal in the entire journey and now this!" Danny expressed his admiration, hardly containing his tears of joy.

"These creatures are extremely stealthy and a challenge even to an experienced hunter. I sometimes spend days searching for one."

"What's your name, sir?"

"You may call me 'Soldier'."

"How did you happen to be in the village this morning? I must say you were godsend. You saved our lives."

"If you want to know the truth," the soldier spoke without lifting his eyes off his work, "I went there to steal a goat. I sneaked into the village very early in the morning, but then I saw the nomads hauling you off to their assembly. I felt obliged to abandon my plan and rescue you."

"They talked about 'the accursed soldier' yesterday. Can it be you that they were talking about?"

"How should I know? They might have been talking about me. What did they say?"

"Nothing much. They thought we might lead them to 'the accursed soldier'."

The soldier cursed between his teeth and focused on his work.

"Had you been to the village before, sir?"

"Yes."

"Why, may I ask?"

"That's none of your business. You ask too many questions. Someone will slit your throat for you if you don't know how to keep your mouth shut."

There was silence for a moment but Danny could not resist asking the next question.

"But is it appropriate to steal from the villagers?"

"The moral principles they teach you at school are applicable only in the school compound. They certainly don't apply here in times like this."

"I tried to steal a goat from the Somalis yesterday."

The soldier lifted up his head and looked at Danny in amazement.

"Where from?"

He told him.

"Wasn't I correct in saying that you two are proper swindlers?"

"Oh, no sir, not both of us. Samuel was against it. I was sick of eating fish. I now realize that it's wrong to steal."

"Why do you say that?"

"I was ungrateful about the daily supply of fish. Stealing was unnecessary."

"You say so because you were unsuccessful. If you had been successful, you'd have thought the opportunity was a godsend. One doesn't feel guilty because one has done something wrong. One feels guilty because one is caught out. In war the vanquished is always the guilty one, the victor, the righteous. It's always been like that since the beginning of time."

"Besides, my mother believed that the Gerimeros love their country and should, therefore, be treated respectfully."

"I'll not insult your mother in front of you, but your mother has no idea what's going on here, does she? Moreover, this has little to do with the Gerimeros. I'd have stolen a goat from anyone had the war been taking place somewhere else. I'm willing to pay for a goat or a sheep or a liter of milk, but the ungrateful villagers won't sell them to us soldiers, because they detest us. So, the only option we have is either to steal or to take them by force."

"Can't you fish? There seem to be enough fish in the river."

The soldier abandoned his work and looked at Danny.

"Are you trying to lecture me about moral values?"

"No, sir."

"Then shut up and hold the legs tight."

The soldier carried on with his work without further conversation. He was skinning the animal while kneeling on one leg. When he had finished detaching the skin, the head, and the hooves from the rest of the body, he stood up.

"Now we have to wake this wet bag up. He has to make the fire," he said, for once his irascible manner giving way to an amiable demeanor. He seemed well pleased with himself.

"Samuel, wake up," Danny gently kicked Samuel in the back with his right foot.

This time Samuel woke up and sat up.

"Do you see?"

"What's that, where did you get it?"

"It's not a goat, mind you and it's not stolen. It's a wild animal the soldier felled with a single bullet."

"Get up and make a fire," the soldier ordered Samuel.

Samuel got up and studied the animal with both disbelief and fascination.

"Aren't you thankful that your life has been saved for the second time in one day?" the soldier addressed Samuel.

"I'm very grateful, sir. Thank you. I'm trying to believe that it's real."

While Samuel prepared the fire, the soldier removed all the internal organs of the animal and wrapped them tightly with the skin along with the head and the hooves.

"We've got to bury these. Remove a folding shovel from the back of the backpack and come along."

Danny did as he was told and followed the soldier down to the river.

"Why don't we throw them into the river? Let the fish and the alligators have something to eat."

"Yes, but someone may also find them and be able to trace back our whereabouts."

He dug a hole in the ground half a meter away from where the river bank began and buried the skin. Afterwards he diligently sprinkled dust on top.

They returned and grilled the meat and ate as much as they could. The soldier carefully wrapped the leftovers in two plastic bags and gave one of them to Samuel.

"You can take it with you tomorrow."

The remainder he put in his backpack. He then removed three Sportsman cigarettes from his backpack and offered two of them to the boys, but they declined.

"Of course, you want to show modesty, which is understandable."

He lit his own cigarettes and put two back into his backpack. Laying himself down on the ground on his back and gazing at the stars, he smoked leisurely. The boys sat beside him and watched him smoke. They were eager to hear his story. But he did not seem to be in the mood for a talk.

"There isn't much to talk about," he said at long last, as if he had read their minds. "A soldier's life is constantly in great danger. A madman has declared war on us, but we are also being ruled by a lunatic. Thousands of soldiers pay with their precious lives on both sides every day, apparently, for nothing. Even the living soldiers die a different sort of death. What will become of the wounded soldiers once the war is over is simply unimaginable. There's nothing attractive about war."

"My father said it's a great honor to die for one's country," Danny declared proudly.

"Your father must be a goddamn propagandist or a compulsive liar. Is your father an officer or a clerk?"

"No, sir, he's a proper infantry soldier." Danny lied.

"There are so many in the military who experience war from a distance. Some pass decisions down from a circular table and some compile statistics in a record office. When your experience of war comes from within the ranks in a bloody battle, when you see your comrades disintegrated by a grenade in front of your eyes, when heads and legs are chopped off within a blink of an eye, then you cannot think of war as anything but cruelty and sheer madness. War has no appeal at all."

"But what will happen if our soldiers refuse to resist the Somali aggressors?" Danny asked him.

"That's the biggest dilemma, isn't it? What will happen if the lunatic leader in Ethiopia wins the war, have you also asked this question?"

"What will happen, sir?"

"You are a proper fool, but I don't blame you for that." There was silence once again and the soldier continued smoking. When he was done, he turned towards Samuel.

"I suppose you're the leader of this odyssey? What's your plan for tomorrow and the days to come?"
"We shall be travelling along the river as usual, sir."
"Following the river all the time can be pretty dangerous. You can easily be tracked. Have you ever been to this place before?"
"Only once, sir."
"When?"
Samuel told him his story for the second time.
"Do you really expect me to believe this pack of lies?"
"But that's the truth, sir."
"As you wish."
The soldier removed a pen and a sheet of paper from his backpack, drew himself near to the fire and invited the boys to come closer. He sketched something resembling the figure of a camel without its legs and tail.
"This is Neghelle," he pointed at the mouth of the camel, "and this one," pointing at the genitals of the camel, he continued, "is where we are, about thirty-five kilometers northeast of Bokolmanyo. Bokolmanyo is about hundred kilometers away from Dolo. The river is represented by the bottom, the back, the hump, the back of the neck, the head, and the face of the camel. The road makes the belly and the neck."

"Do you mean we have travelled hundred kilometers so far?" Danny interrupted with disbelief.

"Yes, or a little more than that."

"That's unbelievable!"

"You two must realize the gravity of the danger you are in. This is not like the sort of adventures you've heard of in fables or read in children's books. Some of the people in this area are hostile and you could be torn to pieces by wild animals at night."

"What is your suggestion, sir?" Samuel asked him.

"I don't have a simple answer. If you go back to Bokolmanyo, you may find a military truck coming from Dolo. But the place will be completely deserted by now and you may fall prey to some vicious home-grown bandits. The next place is Filtu, where there is a proper military camp. If you reach there following the main road, you'll be sheltered and taken care of. But Filtu is very far, approximately, hundred and fifty kilometers from here. There is one more option though, but it involves taking a risk. You'd have to travel along the river for two days, for about fifty kilometers, and then abandon the river and travel westwards, always westwards, for two days. You should be able to come to Filtu. The idea is to avoid this hump. Even if you don't arrive directly at Filtu, you'll arrive at the main road. There's no way you'll miss the road. If you hit the road south of Filtu, then that's fine, you should follow the road northwards until you've arrived at Filtu. If you hit the road north of Filtu, that's still fine, follow the road northwards again and you should come to Udet. There too you'll be helped. Udet is seventy kilometers north of Filtu. The advantage of travelling to Filtu is that the surrounding area is relatively safe. It's too risky for bandits and nomads to lurk in that area where there's a heavy traffic of troops both on ground and in the air. But before you abandon the river, you must have enough supplies of food and drink which should last for three or four days and you should be willing to suffer shortages. The meat I gave you should last for two days or even for three, if you're frugal. You may also find some wild berries on your way. Your main challenge is getting enough water. Unfortunately, I've only one water bottle."

"But there's also the possibility that we'll be lost between the river and Filtu, forever going in circles," Samuel countered.

"That's possible," the soldier attested. "But that's less probable."

"The best option is to follow the river, sir," Samuel responded calmly.

"Best option indeed!" the soldier laughed sarcastically. "No matter which way you opt to take, my advice to you both is to travel only by night and inconspicuously. You haven't done well by travelling in the daytime. Try also to avoid making a fire wherever you can. Fire attracts people as well as wild animals from afar. If you must make a fire, make sure that you are sheltered by something or that the elevation is low. When you rest during the day, stay away from the river. You've already made enemies and they may or may not follow you. If Usman Ali thinks that I'm with you, it's less likely his men will follow you. Still, don't leave anything to chance."

Danny wanted to ask the soldier what his destination was, but he remembered his scolding and put his question aside. The soldier put his things back into his backpack and lay down on the bare ground, fully dressed.

"Just before the day ends, though, I want clarification from both of you for one final time," he said, gazing at the stars. "Let's begin with the big one. You said that your old man was a priest…"

"A prophet, sir," Samuel corrected him.

"Where does he come from?"

"He doesn't have a permanent place to live in. He moves from place to place."

"But where does he come from originally, where did his parents use to live when he was a child?"

"I know that he was an orphan and grew up in a church. He came from the north, but I don't know exactly from which specific place he hailed."

"Is he married, has he his own children?"

"No, sir, he's never been married."

"What does he do exactly?"

"You mean for a living?"

"Didn't you understand my question?"

"It's difficult to explain what he does for a living, sir. I say this because the people to whom I explained our way of life considered it extraordinary. I didn't think that we were at all extraordinary when I was living with him. We used to cultivate our own garden when we stayed in one place long enough. But whenever the prophet felt that his service was needed somewhere else, we abandoned everything and moved on."

"Who gave him the land to cultivate a garden?"

"Why, sir, the country is vast and rich in uncultivated land. We never had a problem finding a piece of land to cultivate."

"Was he a hermit?"

"No, sir. Most of the time he lived amongst people."

"Did you go to school?"

"If you mean in the ordinary sense, no, sir. But the prophet has taught me many things, including how to read and write."

"Damn it, this is all gibberish. Either you were born stupid or pretend to be so. Most probably, you're pretending to be stupid. For what end is the question."

"I've told the truth, sir."

"Blast your truth! How about you, young man. Tell me about your father."

"My father was, is, a soldier," Danny replied.

"What's his rank?"

Danny thought quickly. He wanted to tell the truth but for some reason hesitated. If the soldier knew about his father, that he had been a prominent doctor, he thought, it would make matters complicated. He did not know why he thought so, but he had no time to think everything through calmly and thoroughly. Besides, he could not predict what the consequences the truth might have for Samuel. At that instant, he remembered his father's jacket, which was, indeed, an officer's jacket, and the remark of one of his abductors that very morning.

"My father is a lieutenant," he lied, recalling that the father of one of his schoolmates was a lieutenant.

"In which division?"

"The fourth infantry division."

"Which subdivision?"

"The 27th, sir."

"And your parents live in Neghelle?"

"Yes, sir."

"Which part of the city?"

"We live in 04 Kebele, Senga Tera."

"What's your father's full name?"

Danny told him the full name of his friend's father.

"And your father is stationed in Dolo?"

"Yes, sir."

"Good, I'll find that out. Now, if you excuse me, I must rest. A long journey awaits me tomorrow. Make sure you've extinguished the fire before you sleep."

Consumed by guilt and anxiety Danny looked at Samuel, who also looked mortified.

Chapter 17

The soldier woke the boys very early the next morning, much earlier than they were accustomed to. They both were in deep sleep and opened their eyes with great difficulty.

The soldier was smoking a cigarette, already carrying his backpack on his shoulder. The boys got up with heavy hearts and began to gather their belongings. Silence had always reigned in the wilderness, both by day and by night, but that morning it felt as though they were on a different planet. A waxing crust was floating above in whose faint light the wilderness appeared to be more enigmatic and more frightful than ever. When they were ready, the soldier shook hands with them.

"Well, boys," he spoke with a bass voice, "we have to say farewell to one another now. If we don't see each other in this life again, we shall see each other in heaven, God willing, and assuming there's a heaven. If, there's no heaven, that's also all right. This life is full of troubles and there isn't really much to miss when one dies. You have a difficult and dangerous journey ahead of you. Be brave, be careful, and be cunning, never trust anyone or any place. Don't exhaust your supplies before you have a replacement. My own journey is no less difficult, but I'm called to it."

He gave them some dry biscuits and slices of black bread as well as a box of matches.

"These should bring you closer to Filtu, should you decide to go there. Tread carefully where you go, tread lightly. A careless step and you may sustain an ankle sprain. Fortunately, the ground in this region is relatively even and you should be able to travel without incident. Off you go then. Goodbye."

They shook hands and the boys set off in the faint moonlight.

"You didn't seem very pleased about meeting the soldier. What's the matter?" Danny asked Samuel after they had walked in silence for a while. This had been gnawing at his conscience.

"What's the matter with you!" Samuel retorted peevishly. "Nothing's the matter with me. Aren't you glad that we've been rescued, supplied, taken care of?"

"Well, I am," responded Samuel dismissively.

"You didn't even thank him properly. You've been cool to him throughout. Is it because he used some wrong words?"

"I've been naturally wondering what he's been doing in the wilderness alone while his comrades are fighting the enemy."

"Are you suggesting that he's a traitor?"

"I'm not suggesting anything. I can't help asking the question, can I?"

"It's your life he's rescued, Samuel!"

"And as for you," Samuel stood still suddenly, but hesitated before he spoke. "Yesterday at the assembly you behaved in the strangest manner possible. You were very eager to enter into a fight with the villagers and to see someone get killed in front of you. It seemed to me either you desperately wished to be killed or to kill someone."

"You're jealous because I was braver than you and the soldier praised me for that! Those bastards were ready to torture and kill us. It's regrettable that we didn't see the brains of a couple of those imbeciles blown out. Don't tell me you have compassion for them! As for the soldier, neither of us has any idea what he's been commissioned to do, but he's been good to us. You're being ungrateful. What's the matter with you?"

Samuel resumed going without giving Danny a response. Danny caught up with him feeling angry and hurt.

"Furthermore, you lied to Usman Ali about our parents without first giving me a warning. Why did you do that?"

"Why do you think I lied?"

"I don't know; you'd better tell me."

"Well, I'll tell you why I lied. I lied in order to save your skin! In the light of their hostility, I was anxious for you should I reveal that your father was a prominent military officer. Never mind Usman Ali, you could have told the soldier the truth. Why did you lie to him?"

"I didn't lie to him. I told him the truth."

"No, you didn't tell him the truth.

"He never questioned my account, whereas he questioned yours."

"That doesn't mean you told him the truth. You're a skillful liar, besides."

"I didn't tell him a goddamn lie."

"But you told me that your father was a surgeon."

"But he's also a soldier."

"But you deliberately withheld the most important piece of information, that your father was a military surgeon."

"All, right, I'm a goddamn liar. I'm a skillful liar. I've lied all my life. I inherited it from my father. But you too are a liar! You're no less a sinner," Danny screamed furiously.

"Pull yourself together, nobody blamed you for lying. We both lied because we were afraid. We didn't harm anyone."

It took Danny some time to calm down. Even though Samuel's reproach about his reaction at the assembly had hurt him, deep down, Danny had himself felt uneasiness about his desire to witness bloodshed...

Chapter 18

This secret and awkward desire had been with him for quite some time. Once in Neghelle, there had been a big military event which included different sports and fundraising activities. One afternoon Danny had been watching a football match between two rival clubs. In front of him had been sitting an infantry captain calmly chatting with a beautiful young lady who was sitting next to him.

In the course of the second half of the game, an elderly soldier of a much lower rank came and sat next to the captain and started to shout inordinately, making vulgar comments about the referee. He was properly intoxicated. The captain at first ignored him, but the old man became more and more erratic. At one point, the captain asked the old man to lower his voice, but the old man refused to take heed. Finally, the captain and the lady decided to leave the arena.

As they stood and prepared to leave, however, the old man carelessly blocked the passage with his legs, so that the lady was unable to pass. Whereupon, the captain grabbed him by the collar, lifted him up from his seat and threw him over and beyond the people sitting in the front row. There ensued a huge commotion during which the captain and the lady proceeded to leave the place. When the old man got back on his feet, he brandished a pistol and fired a shot blindly. The captain flew at him and beat him until he was covered with blood. Nobody dared to come between them. The old man finally collapsed on the ground unconscious.

Transfixed in his chair, Danny had watched everything with intense anxiety. At the same time, however, he had been dying to see something unusual, something shocking happening.

"I didn't want to see the captain killed. He'd done everything he could to avoid the fight."

"What did you want to see then?"

"I don't know what I wanted to see."

"Did you want to see the young lady get killed?"

Danny kept silence.

"Were you jealous of the captain?"

"I might have been."

"Was that the first time you had such a feeling?"

"No."

"Well?"

"In Neghelle, the boys resolved disputes with fierce brutality."

"Did you secretly enjoy watching the fights?"

"I might have."

"How unfortunate you are!"

"I once cursed God," Danny confessed unexpectedly.

"What do you mean?" Samuel asked him, turning his face towards him in the dim light.

"I was once arguing with a boy about the existence of God. He tried to convince me that God exists. I challenged him to prove it to me. He couldn't. Then I looked up to the sky and cursed God using very obscene words."

"Simply so?"

"Simply so."

"Whatever induced you to do that?"

"I don't know. But after I'd cursed I couldn't erase the memory from my mind. I wish I hadn't cursed."

"If you show genuine regret, I'm sure God is willing to forgive you."

"You don't understand. I don't believe in the existence of God, but I still wish I hadn't cursed."

"What does it matter, if God doesn't exist?"

"Somehow it matters to me. I shouldn't have cursed."

"I don't see the difference. If there's no God, you haven't offended anyone. So, you shouldn't regret anything. Many people curse the whole day, mostly no one in particular, and they don't seem to regret their actions at all. On the contrary, many are rather pleased with themselves."

"Still, I shouldn't have cursed"

"I don't see the difference."

"I've read a lot about the psychology of cursing. My father used to collect books on human emotions. One of these books had the picture of different people showing different emotions. Underneath each picture there was a brief explanation about the possible causes of the emotion. Underneath "cursing", it says that it's an expression of recognition, rage, helplessness, or rebelliousness, or it is an indirect admission of the significance of the person or the thing being cursed. Have you ever thought about this?"

"So you mean, with your cursing, you were indirectly acknowledging the existence of God?"

"Correct."

"So, you're upset because there's a contradiction between your belief and action?"

"You see my point."

"But now since the action is a thing of the past, you should forget about it."

"I'm not very good at forgetting."

"This is because you haven't forgiven yourself."

"My father said that it was easier for me to nurse my grievances than do something about them."

"It's true, some people find pleasure in nursing their wounds."

"It's one thing to say I should do something about my grievances, but it's another to show what I should do about them. I was a sickly boy all my life and there was nothing I could do about it."

"But you can do something about it. You can let go of your grievances. You can learn to love. There's liberty in love, my old man used to say."

"But how? Do you think I'm comfortable with my grievances? I'm sick of them."

"Healing begins with the mind. You can begin by disowning your grievances."

"You mean I should assign ownership of my grievances to something else, like, to the Devil? I don't believe in the Devil, you know."

"What I mean is that you can refuse to be irked about the past. Even if you can't do anything else, your refusal alone can be a miracle."

"I don't understand a thing you say. The soldier is right in saying you're an enigma. You speak so easily and so finely because you have no idea about suffering."

Samuel refrained from making a response. They walked in silence. Danny tried to comprehend Samuel's last statement.

"There's something else," he broke the silence at long last.

"What is it?"

"My mother once took me to the countryside to visit a relative. It was a market day and there was a big market in front of the house. In the middle of our visit, I went to the backyard, collected a big stone, and threw the stone from behind at the market goers."

"No!"

"Yes."

"I don't believe you!"

"You'd better believe me, because I'm telling you the truth."

"Whatever induced you to do that?"

"I don't know. Nothing in particular. Maybe I was bored, I cannot say what precisely induced me to throw a stone at innocent and unsuspecting people. But I remember to this day, every single detail of it, how I threw the stone. After I'd thrown the stone I panicked and had a terrible cough attack, but that day I didn't faint. I remained conscious."

"Did you go out and see whether you'd hurt anyone?"

"No."

"Did you tell your mom what you'd done?"

"No, I didn't. This is the first time I've spoken about it."

"How old were you?"

"This happened three years ago, when I was eleven years old."

"It must have been a great burden on you to keep this inside all this time."

"It has been."

"Maybe nobody was injured."

"Maybe. Maybe somebody was injured really badly. The stone was big."

"It's a thing of the past, you can't do anything about it now."

"Which is why I'm furious. I can't change anything."

"But you can decide to be good."

"Most of the things I've done in the past were not good."

"At least you don't need anyone to convince you that you're a sinner."

"There's another thing I want to tell you about."

"Go on, tell me."

Danny hesitated for a moment but decided to tell him.

"There was this nasty boy at school who used to rankle me a lot on account of a girl. He had neither father nor mother and earned money by transporting heavy items for people after school. The imbecile had his own gang already. One evening I watched him having a serious bicycle accident in a heavy rain. There was nobody around except me. He cried for help, because he'd smashed his knee."

"Did you help him?"

"No. I just left him there."

"What happened to him?"

Danny sighed deeply.

"He managed to drag himself into somebody's house."

"Did he recover?"

"I don't know. I never saw him again."

"How did you know that he'd managed to drag himself into somebody's house?"

"I knew all right."

There was a long silence.

"You feel terrible about the incident, don't you?"

"Very much," Danny retorted with a hoarse voice. "I was a coward, after all, in leaving a helpless boy on the street."

Samuel was thoughtful for a while.

"If this is the true cause of your pain, then you have a noble heart."

"Are you making fun of me?"

"Not at all. You might have acted like a coward, but you detested being a coward. The two are very different."

"I've always been haunted by the fear of being a coward."

"Indeed, being a coward is something to be bothered about."

"But it's very frustrating to find myself acting like a coward time and again. It hurts a lot."

"I understand you. I myself struggle to be brave. Sometimes I succeed, sometimes I don't. It's a constant struggle, you know. We mustn't give up."

"I sometimes meet boys at school who behave honorably and do well without much effort. I've never done anything good without an effort."

"You can never tell whether someone has done something good effortlessly. A good deed cannot be done effortlessly, if you ask me."

"But I do evil things most of the time. I also lie a lot. I lie even when it's not necessary, you know, even when I'm not forced or threatened. Just for the heck of it. I often think that my true illness is lying. Sometimes it shocks me how easily I lie."

"As long as we don't feel at home with our weaknesses, there's a hope of vanquishing some of them. However, we should keep on trying to overcome evil. Half the victory in fighting evil lies in our trying, so the prophet taught me." Danny was silent. He suddenly felt weary and sad. He had hardly realized how taxing the confession had been on his emotional energy.

Chapter 19

They travelled undisturbed until morning and then decided to take a break until sundown. Moving deliberately away from the river to the west, they spent some time searching for a suitable place of rest. When they finally found a place surrounded by dusty bushes about half a kilometer away from the river, they settled for it.

"We should sleep now and eat later when we wake up," Samuel suggested.

"Why can't we eat now?"

"You go ahead and eat, if you're hungry."

Danny did not understand Samuel but had no energy to complain or argue. They spread their jackets on the dusty ground in the shade and lay down. They fell asleep almost instantly, but after a while Samuel suddenly woke up.

"I heard a noise!" he whispered in Danny's ear.

Danny too awoke in alarm.

"What noise?" he asked and stood up.

"Didn't you hear a noise? There was a noise, I'm sure of it."

"What noise?" Danny repeated.

"I thought I heard something. Didn't you hear anything?"

"I might have heard something, but I'm not sure."

They both stood up and, protected by the bushes, looked around carefully. But they could not see anything.

"Do you think we're being followed?" Danny whispered.

"Possibly. We have to leave the bushes and go out into the open, just to be safe."

They emerged cautiously from the bushes and scanned the vast and barren territory all around them. There was nothing to be seen far and wide, except for dusty and skeletal bushes and naked anthills. Nevertheless, neither of them felt safe.

"What shall we do now?" Danny asked.

"I went to sleep afraid of being followed. Perhaps the noise came from within my own mind. Try to think clearly, did you hear a noise or not?"

"I might have, I'm not sure. As soon as you spoke about a noise, I thought I might have heard a noise, but I can't be sure. Let's go and rest."

They returned to the bushes and lay down but neither one was able to sleep.

"Let me go and fetch water," Danny suggested.

He stood up and collected the water bottle and went to the river. It was not really because they needed water that he wanted to go. He wanted to overcome his fear. He went to the river cautiously, without hurrying, filled the water bottle, leisurely rinsed his feet in the river and came back, feeling proud of himself. Samuel was already lying down, half closing his eyes, almost asleep.

"You're back?" he mumbled with a weak voice and closed his eyes.

Danny did not answer him. Instead, he put the water bottle down next to Samuel's bag and lay down himself. It was a quiet, hot and windless day. Despite the confidence he had felt a while ago, he now felt oppressed by the silence and the stillness encompassing them.

"Sound is a true miracle," he thought.

He remembered there was a time when he considered light the truest miracle of all, for as a child, he had been afraid of darkness.

"Wherever life reigns, there is sound," he thought. "There are plenty of places where there is light but no life. Mars, for example. Was I terrified of silence rather than darkness when I was a child? I'd rather be amongst people, where there are loud cheers and laughter, than be alone."

At long last, he too slumbered.

In less than ten minutes or so, however, Samuel suddenly woke up for the second time.

"There's that noise again!" he retorted.

Danny woke up almost instantly and sat up.

"What now?"

Samuel looked at Danny questioningly.

"Didn't you hear the noise?"

"What noise? You heard a noise again?"

"You didn't hear it?"

"How did it sound?"

"Difficult to describe. It was a mixture of clattering and hissing. You're sure you didn't hear it?"

"I'm not sure," replied Danny feeling uneasy.

"Someone is lurking around, I'm quite sure."

They stood up for the second time and looked around, but there was no one to be seen.

"Are you sure, you heard a noise?" Danny asked.

"Yes, I'm sure."

"Are you sure you haven't had a bad dream this time?"

"I am sure."

"Strange."

They emerged from the bushes and went out into the open and surveyed their surroundings carefully. They went to the nearby anthills and looked around them to make sure nobody was hiding behind them. There was no one to be seen or found. They went into the shade and rested, but felt so unsafe that they were talking in whispers and looking right and left repeatedly as they talked. Overwhelmed by weariness and anxiety, however, they slumbered, but for the third time Samuel awoke suddenly. "We have to leave this place," he said decidedly. "We must abandon the river altogether and go eastwards."

"You mean westwards?"

"No, no, no, I mean eastwards. If those villagers have decided to follow us, they'll be coming either from the south or from the southwest. They know that the main road and the military camps lie to the west of the river. They'll think that we'll eventually head towards the camps. They've already taken us for spies, don't forget. By now they most certainly think that the coming of the soldier at the last minute to rescue us was premeditated. They'll have figured all of this out by now. If we go westwards, we'll fall into their trap."

"But if they think we were working for the soldier, it's unlikely they'll follow us."

"But they'll also have anticipated that the soldier had other pressing things to take care of and therefore couldn't be with us all the time."

"I guess you're right. But how far should we diverge from the river?"

"Far enough. Staying near the river makes us vulnerable. Remember, they're many in number. They can search a wide area at the same time."

"Samuel, you're exaggerating a little. Even if we assume that your fear is well-founded, we shall die of thirst if we abandon the river."

"That's a possibility we'll have to reckon with, but for now we have no other option. Listen, we can discuss this as we travel. Now we have to move cautiously but quickly. As soon as we reach the river, you swim first and then I'll follow."

"You can go ahead and swim first."

"We'll throw all our belongings over the river but we should swim with all our clothes on."

"I can't swim with the jacket on."

"All right, we'll put the jackets in my bag and throw the bag and my staff over."

"Look, there's no one around. There's no need to be alarmed."

"We must travel as far away from the river as possible before it gets dark."

They crossed the river but Danny lingered, unable to reconcile himself with the idea of abandoning the river for an unknown and a much less certain destination, whereas Samuel was impatient to leave the place.

"Hurry up, we must leave this place at once!"

Danny remembered this urgency in Samuel's voice. He had spoken with the same degree of urgency when they first had met. Back then he had decided to follow Samuel having no idea who he was and having no clear idea where their odyssey would lead or end. Yet, Samuel's proposal to abandon Dolo and Danny's decision to follow Samuel had not entirely been irrational. Now his heart was throbbing at the prospect of abandoning Ganale, the river which had supplied them with practically everything they needed to stay alive. Was this not a heedless invitation to a slow and painful death?

Samuel curtailed his movement and looked back.

"I know what's going on in your mind and I understand you. But we have to make a decision. I can't stay here. I'm determined to carry out my plan. If you're afraid, carry on your way without me."

"You're out of your mind," Danny yelled in frustration. "We'll surely die if we abandon the river. There's no way we'll find water in this dry and dusty place anywhere other than here."

"I can't live in fear. Our pursuers understand our dependency on the river. It's only a question of time before they capture us if we stick to the idea of staying by the river."

"I just hope that you'll realize at some point that it was a mistake to abandon the river. If this happens, will you be willing to return as quickly as possible?"

"I can't give you a definite answer now. I can't make a promise."

"Why not?"

"I'm almost certain that abandoning the river is the best decision we can make at present."

Danny could not believe what he had heard.

"How can you be sure?"

"It's difficult to explain this to you."

"Why?"

"Because there are certain things you may not be able to understand."

"I'm only two years younger than you. I might have been sickly in the past, but that doesn't mean I'm stupid."

"I didn't mean you're stupid."

"So, if I'm not stupid, why can't I understand?"

"It's not just that you may not be able to understand my explanation. I may also not be able to make myself comprehensible."

"Let me ask you a question, but please tell me the truth."

"Go on."

"What are you really up to, I mean what is your mission? Where are you going, I mean in the end? What are you searching for?"

"You said one question, but that's three."

"Answer me, please."

"Are you beginning to question your faith in me?"

"I just want to know the truth."

"If you really want to know the truth, the prophet has taught me since I was a child to listen to an inner voice. When he was still with me, I used to get confirmation from him every now and then. Since I lost him, I've become less reliant upon the inner voice. But today, I have reason to believe that this voice is strong and persistent. If I ignore it, I'll be unhappy. I'm not asking you to understand me. You're free to obey your own conscience."

"What inner voice are you talking about?"

"I know this sounds like foolishness to you."

"Earlier it was a noise we were talking about, now we're talking about an inner voice."

"The two aren't entirely unrelated."

"I can't walk away. I'd be lost without you. You persuaded me to follow you and now here I am. You should accept some responsibility for my present condition. It's irresponsible of you to abandon a friend in the middle of nowhere or to oblige him to take an unknown and dangerous path."

"If you want us to stick together, you must trust me."

"But how can you know that you have heard an inner voice, what is the sign?"

"It's difficult to explain unless you yourself have experienced it before."

"Why didn't the inner voice tell you where to meet the prophet in the first place, if you are accustomed to hearing it?"

"It's difficult to answer this question. The inner voice gives hints and clues. It takes faith to make a connection between them. The stronger my faith, the more hints and clues I'm able to discover and the less difficult it becomes for me to make sense of them. It's like a word game, if you think about it."

"But life is no puzzle," Danny rebutted once again. "We're at a crossroads. It's a matter of life or death, what we're about to decide."

"I'm asking you to trust me."

"You're incomprehensible to me."

"There's no point discussing this matter any further. This is not how I wish to exist. I insist that we split up. You go your way and I go mine."

"I see!" Danny screamed in great anguish, his eyes suddenly filled with hot tears. It just occurred to him that perhaps Samuel was seeking an occasion to part company with him at any cost.

"You're upset with me. You're upset with my reaction at the assembly and with all the stories I told you. You want to part company with me because you think I'm a bad boy."

"What are you talking about?" Samuel screamed back.

"Please don't lie to me. It'd be hypocritical of you to lie or pretend. It's as clear as day to me now."

"No, no, no, you don't understand," Samuel came closer and put his right hand on Danny's left shoulder. "What I told you is the truth. I want you to come with me, but I cannot force you to come with me."

"I'll come with you, no matter what the cost!" Danny replied firmly.

"Will you?"

"Yes."

"I'm so glad. I'd have regretted it if you'd decided otherwise."

"If I must die, I'd rather die with you."

"You're a faithful friend. Now, let's hurry."

For a long time, they progressed onwards setting their sight on a remote hill in front of them and searching at the same time for a proper footpath. But there was no footpath. The ground was barren and dusty.

"Can we eat something?" Danny called out in bitterness. He was trailing five or six meters behind Samuel.

"Let's eat some of the grilled meat," Samuel agreed and waited for Danny.

They rested on the bare ground in the sun and divided amongst themselves some grilled ribs. Both of them were already thirsty and sweating a lot, but they restrained themselves from drinking too much water.

"This is unbearable," Danny bemoaned. "What are we going to do when we've finished the water?"

"I don't know; I don't really know. But we should find some water today."

"In this place?"

"Where else?"

Danny chuckled bitterly and took a bite. The soldier must have been skillful in grilling the meat, because, even though many hours had already passed since the meat had been grilled, it was still tasty and juicy.

Chapter 20

After they had eaten, they decided to continue resting for a little longer.

"There's something I didn't tell you about," said Danny after a moment of hesitation, fixing his eyes on the ground.

"What is it?"

"Do you remember how we met on the first day, on the hill?"

"Of course."

"When I saw the jet dashing towards the medical facility, I felt momentary gladness that my father and his mistress would be killed."

"Did your father have a mistress?"

"Yes. She was like a big sister to me."

Samuel was taken aback by this sudden confession, so much so that he did not immediately know what to say. He looked at Danny with his lips parted. As soon as Danny had made the confession, he felt sad and tears began rolling down his cheeks.

"How did your … eh, the woman, you know whom I'm referring to, come to Dolo?"

"My dad found a nursing job for her a year ago."

"She was a nurse?"

"She grew up in our house," Danny went on, ignoring Samuel's question. "She came to us when she was ten and I was five years old. My father brought her from his birthplace, because she was an orphan and she had no other relatives. My mom brought her up as her daughter. The two understood each other very much. She was like a big sister to me."

"It's difficult to imagine," Samuel mumbled knowing not what to say.

"That's what I've been thinking all this time."

"What was your father like?"

"He was a great surgeon, you know, everybody said so," Danny began, fresh tears rolling down his cheeks. "His dream was to become a famous professor of surgery. But when he was studying at the university, he and his friends opposed the Emperor and went out onto the streets to protest. At that time some generals tried to overthrow the Emperor, but their plan failed and the generals were hunted down and hanged in public. My father and his friends were forced to abandon their studies and to go into hiding. My father hid in a village near Neghelle where my mother and her family were living. He agreed to work for my grandfather and there he met and fell in love with my mom. Later they got married. But one day, word reached their ears that some informants had revealed my father's identity to the authorities. My parents fled from there and moved to another place, and from there to yet another place. They did that for three years. Finally, my father changed his name and joined the army, because he thought it was the least likely place to be discovered. But there he was discovered, all the same, and was put in prison for three years. When he was released from prison, he was permitted to finish his studies on condition that he work for the military. He was hoping to be released from his obligation one day, so that he could pursue an academic career. Then the revolution erupted and he never got the chance to go back to university. He lived the rest of his life with the regret of not going back to university."

"Was he happy at home?"

"Not really. He was happier when there was war or some instability in the region. Then he had something to occupy his mind with. When there was no war, he felt bored and restless. After work and at weekends he would spend most of the time at home planting and uprooting trees in the garden, renovating the house, or destroying and rebuilding fences. In the evening he would go out with his friends and come home very late completely drunk. Then he would fight with mom and beat her. One time, he even fired at her with his pistol and nearly killed her. When the fight was over, mom would leave him and go to her parents, taking us with her, and spend a long time there. Then he would come after her and beg her to come home with him. We would have some peace for a while and then everything would repeat itself all over again."

"Did you have a good relationship with him?"

"I don't really know whether he liked me or not. I think he liked me but was upset because I was a sick and fragile boy. My father read a lot and encouraged me to read. When he was sober, we talked about books a lot. He always talked to me like an adult, which I liked very much. But when he was drunk, he never wanted me to be around. He was jealous of my mom. That was why they fought most of the time. He never trusted her even though he was the one who was unfaithful. My mom is very pretty, you know, and sociable. She is very funny and generous, besides. My father didn't like any of those things about her."

"And what about you, did you like your father?"

"What a question you ask!"

Saying this, Danny kept quiet for some time. He was palpably upset.

"I don't hate my father," he said at length. "I'm only sorry for him. He shouldn't have done it with Zema, though."

"Who is Zema?"

"My adoptive sister."

"Do you feel guilty because you wished him dead?"

"I suppose."

"You couldn't have prevented the bombing."

"I know."

"Besides, he had acted irresponsibly."

"I know that too."

"We all are responsible for our actions."

"Do you think so? Are we responsible if someone murders us here in the wilderness?"

"Our lives are in the hands of God."

"Aren't you contradicting yourself?"

"God has given us freedom, so that we can enjoy a relationship with him. Love is not possible without freedom. Where there is freedom, there is also responsibility. At the same time, however, our freedom isn't beyond God's sphere of influence. If God left us to our freedom entirely, there'd be no second-chances, no learning, no growing, no thankfulness, nor, in short, love. So, you see, there is a magical circle going around, connecting love, freedom, and intervention."

"My father believed that human existence is purposeless."

"I'm not surprised. Much had been missing from his life."

"Do you believe that our life has a purpose?"

"Don't you believe that?"

"I asked you first."

"Our life has a purpose, I have no doubt, but we may not be able to discover it completely so long as we are in it. The reason we ask whether or not our life has a purpose is because we're unhappy. Happy people don't ask such a question."

"How do you know life has a purpose?"

"Suppose you're swimming in an ocean which you'd never seen from above or from afar. You know that you're swimming in a vast and magnificent ocean, but you may not be able to tell its exact depth, breadth, and length as long as you are in it. Life is much bigger than an ocean."

"Life is a great burden, full of suffering."

"But that doesn't mean it has no purpose. Suffering comes from the absence of peace. The question should be how to restore peace and not to deny its existence."

"Why should someone put me in an ocean without my consent?"

"Well, that's what we should live for, to find out why we exist. But if we wish to discover the truth, we should also lead a truthful life. We can't discover the truth about life if we don't pursue the truth."

"Do you think it'll be the end of us if we perish in the wilderness?"

"The wilderness is neither our beginning nor our end."

"Do you think there's life after death?"

"Why do you ask? Are you afraid that we may die in the wilderness?"

"Aren't you?"

"Well, I am."

"And?"

"It isn't by endeavor that we learn to value our lives, the prophet used to say. It's a gift."

"You're full of riddles, Samuel, and you're only sixteen."

"For a person who hasn't learned how to read, a book is a great riddle. But for the one who can decipher it, its words, verses, and poetry are delightful."

"So you mean I'm uneducated?"

"We all are uneducated, if you think about it. Life's our school."

"Aren't you afraid of death?"

"I'm afraid of dying."

"And death?"

Samuel did not answer immediately.

"Well?"

"Shall I tell you a story? It's a little long, though."

"A story about what?"

"The fear I once had."

"I'm ready to listen."

"When I was ten years old, the prophet and I came to a certain town to spend the summer there. Our place was in a quiet corner on the outskirts of the town. Apart from an old house next to ours there were no other houses nearby. But this house was big and surrounded on all sides with a wooden fence. Behind the fence, we could see a large number of tall and leafy mango trees, full of mangos. In this house was living a lonely and mysterious man. On the day we arrived, the prophet told me to avoid him, saying that the man was irascible and dangerous. During our entire stay, I never saw anyone coming into or going out of the house. The man himself could rarely be seen. One late afternoon, though, as the prophet and I were preparing to go out for a walk, we heard successive gunshots and the screaming of boys. We were startled, but then I decided to rush out and see what had happened. But I was forbidden to go out. Later, the prophet told me that the man had fired at some boys who had tried to scale his fence in order to steal mangos. Fortunately, nobody was hurt. Some days passed and I nearly forgot the incident. Then one late evening, as I was playing outside by myself, the man suddenly came out of nowhere and asked me what I was doing. I was so petrified that I was unable to give him an answer. He repeated his question. This time I mustered the courage and told him that I was living there. 'You are lurking here to steal mangos; leave this place now,' he ordered me. I tried to explain that I had no intention of stealing his mangos, but he cut me short and demanded that I leave at once. Recalling the gunshots, the boys screaming, and the prophet's warning, I cautiously left the place and went inside. The prophet wasn't in the house, so I kept on thinking: What if the man doesn't believe me, that I'm living here? What if he decides to come after me and shoot me? I closed all the doors and the windows and waited in great anxiety and suspense, but the man didn't come. When the prophet came back, I told him everything. The following day we left that town and moved to another place. From that day on, whenever I was distressed or anxious or when it was too hot in the room and there was no fresh air, I used to dream of that man pursuing and shooting at me from behind. Four years passed and one day the prophet announced that we were going back to that same town. I reminded him about the man, but he simply replied that the man was no longer a menace. Still, I couldn't get the man out of my mind and from that day on I started to have bad dreams once again. A few weeks later we moved to the town and took up a new residence in a house which wasn't very far from our old house. Despite my terror of encountering the man, I couldn't resist the desire to go and see the old house. One afternoon, after much thought and consideration, I finally decided to go to the old house. On the way, however, I met the prophet talking with a short elderly man and he asked me where I was going. When I told him, he gestured in the direction of the old man and said: 'You remember, of course, our old neighbor.' I couldn't remember him. 'He was our neighbor at the old house, the one you were afraid of.' I studied the old man carefully, unable to believe my eyes. This man was two heads shorter than I and looked very sick and frail. He had no eyelashes or eyebrows and his eyes looked very small and frightened in their sockets. The man extended a shriveled hand and we shook hands. Then I left them wondering whether this was really the same man on account of whom I had had so many bad dreams."

"But what's the relationship between death and the story?"

"You see, all the time I was dreading the man, he'd been portrayed in my mind as though he was outside of time, as though he would never age, never grow tired or weary."

"But what has this got to do with death?"

"Old Death is not outside of time, either, and time itself is a creation. When the power of time comes to an end, Old Death itself will be destroyed."

"I don't understand."

"The prophet once told me that the true miracles in creation are ideas. You see, when we think of freedom, love, infinity, dimension, gravity, limitation, time, pain, death, eternity, and even life, they are all ideas. God first created ideas and then the things by which they can be manifested. But we all consider ideas to be immutable and judge the rationality of every argument in terms of them. But even ideas, including the ideas of rationality and permanence, are subject to God. They have no power of their own."

"I suppose I understand what you mean. All the same, I'm afraid of death. I've been afraid of death all my life. I can't help being afraid of death."

"When life takes root in you, you'll have a purpose for which you will live or die. Then death will cease to frighten you."

Chapter 21

After Samuel had spoken these words, he stood up, ready to go. Danny followed his lead with a heavy heart. They resumed their journey towards the remote hill desperately hoping to discover a small river or a well on their way, but they could not find any. The only sign of life they could see around them were the sporadic bushes, most of which were dry and leafless. The farther away they headed away from the river, the more perturbed Danny became lest they lost orientation and might never be able to get back to the river.

But Samuel pressed on, and Danny followed him with diminishing patience. The consciousness that soon the water in the bottle would run out was consuming him. For the first time in his life, he began to pray silently to the God whose existence he had hitherto never acknowledged. Around two o'clock in the afternoon, his legs refused to cooperate and he stumbled twice, narrowly avoiding injury. The third time he fell down next to a skeletal bush and refused to get up.

"I can't go on," he whined, tears flowing down his cheeks, and spat on the ground, sick of the persistent taste of sweat on his lips.

"All right, we shall take a break here," Samuel consented. They sat down on the bare ground once again and pulled their jackets over their heads to protect themselves from the sun.

"Go ahead, drink a little." Samuel passed Danny the water bottle.

Danny took two successive sips, greedily, only restraining himself with great difficulty. The water was hot and the bottle was more than half empty now. Samuel took a slice of grilled meat from his bag and offered it to Danny.

"Aren't you going to eat and drink?"

"I can wait."

"Then I'm not going to eat."

"Don't be silly. Go ahead and eat, otherwise, you'll fall ill and become a great burden to me. I'm used to fasting for days at a time from my experience of travelling with the prophet."

Danny ate and lay down on the ground, covering himself with his father's jacket and fell asleep immediately. He slept for an hour and woke up with a scorching thirst. Samuel was lying down next to him on his stomach, covered with his jacket. He seemed to have an uneasy sleep, for he was mumbling something in his sleep.

Unable to withstand the temptation, Danny cautiously reached for the water bottle and took a mouthful. After the first mouthful he was no longer able to restrain himself, so took two more mouthfuls before putting the bottle back. He lay down on his side and closed his eyes, wishing to fall back to sleep. His mind was acutely alert, nonetheless, and busy with questions which were at once nonsensical and infuriating. He shifted sides and finally threw his jacket aside and settled lying down on his back, staring blankly at the vast blue sky.

Meanwhile, Samuel, oscillating between wakefulness and sleepiness, was having a dream. In his dream, he saw Roi walking past them, towards the far hill in the east.

"Still searching for the Tree of Strength?" he called out, somehow this time aware of dreaming about her.

Roi stopped tentatively and looked back.

"I've come thus far, as you see," she answered with a small smile playing on her lips.

"Last time you left without saying goodbye," he remarked reproachfully.

"Time doesn't have a single dimension only in the wilderness, you should know this by now."

"Were you following us?"

"Why should I follow you? Or do you think that I was following you because I was behind you?"

"I don't know."

"Stop thinking in a single dimension only."

Roi prepared to resume her journey.

"But where are you off to now? Please stay for a short while," Samuel tried to get up, but he was unable to do so.

"I must make haste," Roi replied without turning back.

"You and your friend, where is your destination?"

"We have no destination, for now."

"We all have a destination. Some know their destination earlier than others. This time it's you who's having doubts. As it were, no one is strong enough not to fall down and no one is weak enough not to rise up again."

"Well, then, goodbye."

Roi resumed her journey and Samuel struggled to get up. Then he heard Danny calling his name and he stood up immediately.

"We must have been travelling south the entire time, look where the sun stands," Danny pointed at the sun.

The remark did not interest Samuel. Looking gloomy, he fixed his eyes on the remote hill and remained standing.

"What's the matter?"

"This morning I could almost certainly hear the inner voice, but now my confidence is shaken. I'm perplexed and feel abandoned."

"Is it the first time that you've felt abandoned? We've been abandoned all the time. Didn't your prophet abandon you a long time ago?"

"Don't talk like that, please."

"So, we should return to the river," Danny jumped to his feet and began collecting his father's jacket. But Samuel remained standing.

"Why are you lingering? It'll be dark soon and our water bottle is nearly empty."

"Oh, leave me alone!"

"Leave you alone, Samuel?" Danny yelled at him. "Do you want us to perish in the wilderness, what's the matter with you?"

Samuel walked back and forth in exasperation.

"This," he said finally, pausing his movement, "is what I think and this is what I'll do, even if it sounds like madness to you. If the man I've been serving is indeed a prophet, nothing will happen to me without the knowledge of God he serves. But if my dreams and my plans are unknown to God or are hidden from him, then I have spent my whole life in deception. In that case life and death are all the same to me. I'll not return to the river."

Danny could not believe what he had just heard. His old anger suddenly rose in him with frightful intensity. He was not only exasperated but also felt betrayed.

'Something is definitely wrong with him!' he could not help thinking at that instant.

Was Samuel suffering from some mental illness? Had the long and dreadful journey and their encounter with the nomads and their coming face to face with death affected his mind? Danny knew soldiers who had had traumatic experiences of war. Some of them had ended up becoming extremely violent and some of them suicidal. If Samuel was out of his mind and not accountable for his actions, what was he supposed to do?

"You do think I'm out of my mind, don't you? I can see it from the horror in your eyes. But don't worry, I'm of sound mind."

"I don't know what to think of you," Danny confessed, subduing his temper. "But you're correct in saying I'm terrified. This place is not to be trifled with. It has exhausted our strength and we've consumed almost all our supplies. If we waste another day in the wilderness without water, why, you may rest assured that we'll die of weakness if not of illness."

"You were wasting away when I found you, but now look at you. Despite all the ordeals we have endured, you look fine."

"I hate my life."

"So what's your decision?"

"What decision or choice am I left with? It all depends on you. I can't go anywhere without you."

Samuel collected his belongings without saying another word and set off in the same direction they had followed in the morning. Danny likewise picked up his jacket and followed him.

They travelled without having any destination in my mind, but Samuel still pressed on as if his very existence depended on this journey. As they approached the hill from a distance, the landscape began to turn faintly greener and gently steeper. It took them about an hour and a half to arrive at the foot of the hill. There, Samuel waited for Danny who was trailing far behind.

"We shall ascend the hill and take another break on top. If the place is convenient, we can spend the night there," Samuel suggested when Danny joined him. "The Prophet often sojourns on top of a mountain or a hill. It used to irritate and exasperate me when I was young, but as I grew older, I began to enjoy the serenity and the view from above."

Danny looked at Samuel with murderous eyes and carried on silently. Nevertheless, he could not help noticing how tired and ghostly Samuel looked and felt sorry for him. Samuel followed him. The hill looked modest from afar but it took them approximately another twenty minutes to reach at the top. Then Samuel threw himself on the ground. Danny removed the water bottle and emptied the water with one gulp and threw himself next to Samuel. They lay down on the ground on their back, Danny closing his eyes. Both of them were awake, dreadfully aware of the passing of every second and minute and the certainty of the coming of darkness and a damning night.

"Whatever is going to happen?" Danny asked himself for the hundredth time.

"I see birds," he heard Samuel's soft voice.

Danny did not react. He did not care.

"I see many birds flying in a line," Samuel repeated, forcing himself to a sitting position.

"Are you afraid that they'll attack us?" Danny asked with a faint voice without opening his eyes.

"It's strange to see so many birds in the middle of nowhere. They're not here by accident, I dare say!"

Danny was too weak to respond.

"You don't understand. This is strange. So many birds in such a desolate place! What are they doing here? They must have found something. Come, let's go and discover what they've found."

"Don't tell me you're curious," Danny forced himself to say. "I've no strength left for curiosity."

"We must go and find out!" Samuel insisted and stood up.

"Where should we go?" Danny wanted to yell, but having no strength left, uttered the words feebly.

"To the other side of the hill."

Danny raised his head and saw Samuel going towards the side of the hill which was perpendicular to the direction from which they had come. He hesitated for a moment but with great annoyance decided to follow him. From where they had been, it was about a hundred-meter distance to that side of the hill.

When Samuel reached at the other end, he saw below a thin, brownish line winding around the foot of the hill. He had no doubt it was a river. For a second or two he thought he was hallucinating. He involuntarily blinked three times, but the thin brown line was still there bracing the hill at its foot.

"Oh, Danny," he screamed, tears of joy suddenly flooding his eyes, "it looks like we've found a river. We're saved Danny! Look what we've found!"

He descended the hill at terrific pace, paying no heed to his own safety. Danny followed him gathering all the strength he could harness. This side of the hill was completely barren and they could see unhindered in all directions. When they were below the middle of the hill, something else captured their attention. They saw a man jumping on a black horse and fiercely galloping away from them, northwards along the river. He was holding the reins in his right hand and brandishing a rifle in his left. His torso was completely bare.

"Did you see that man?" Samuel shouted.

Danny had seen him.

"Hey, you! Will you stop for a moment, please?" Samuel shouted out on the top of his voice but the wind carried his voice away.

"What was he up to? Has he seen us?"

"I suppose he has seen us," Danny responded from behind. The boys hurried to the river but as they came closer, something else caught their attention. On the flat surface of a big rock standing a little away from the river, towards the foot of the hill, they could see someone lying down. It appeared to be a boy of approximately Danny's age, judging from his size, completely naked and with his hands and feet fettered with a rope.

Samuel was the first to arrive and climb up onto the rock. The boy's mouth was tightly gagged and he lay motionless.

"A dead boy!" Samuel announced gravely.

"What's happened to him?" Danny inquired as he approached the rock.

"Come quickly and see."

"Damn it, Samuel, what's happened to him?"

"The man must have killed him."

"Is he bleeding?"

"No."

Danny climbed onto the rock with great patience and stared at the boy with a great shock.

"Are you sure he's dead?" he asked in a hoarse voice.

Danny knelt down and listened to his heartbeat.

"He's not dead," he said.

Samuel, too, checked his pulse and confirmed that the boy was still alive.

"He's unconscious, though."

"I wonder what the man was trying to do to him."

"He was about to kill him, there's no doubt about that. He was about to slaughter him."

"Oh, God! What a brute!"

"We must set him free at once, Danny. I'll untie his hands. You free his mouth."

Danny obeyed.

"We should take him to the water and cool his body with water. The sun has scorched his body."

"Let's hurry up then."

"I now realize that I was sent to rescue this boy. I hope I'm not too late. I should have rushed at once. I've lingered so many times unnecessarily."

"Come on, Samuel, this is not your fault."

"How can we transport him to the river?"

Samuel removed his T-shirt and shorts and dressed the boy. He himself was now wearing only his underwear.

"What a barbaric act! What an unfortunate boy!" Danny muttered and added, "Who do you think the man was and why did he do it?"

"I've no idea who he could be and why he wanted to commit such a horrible crime."

"I've been warned by my father and other soldiers in Neghelle of dangerous people lurking in our town intending to kidnap boys and do terrible things to them. I never believed them, though. I now see that they were telling the truth. I thought they were merely trying to frighten us and to prevent us from leaving the town on our own. Some of the boys were fond of hunting. Do you think he'll recover?"

"I don't know. Apparently he's dehydrated. It's likely that he hasn't eaten or drunk anything for many hours. We must bring him to the river and wet his lips with water."

"It's a miracle that we found him."

"Yes, it's a miracle."

"Was he really trying to slaughter him?" Danny asked indignantly.

"Most certainly."

"Where are his clothes?"

"The man must have taken them with him or has hidden or buried them somewhere."

"Do you think he was abducted?"

"What do you mean? You mean he came here freely and that the man was Father Abraham?"

"You never know."

"Enough with the twaddle, we have to transfer him to the river."

"But how can we transfer him?"

"I'll climb down and prepare myself to carry him on my back. You should hold him under his armpits and gently slide him onto my back."

"Are you sure that's a good idea? One of us might drop him and hurt him."

"We have no other option."

At that instant they heard a voice calling from below.

"Well, well, well, who do we have here?"

In shock, they turned their faces towards the voice and looked down. It was the very same soldier who had saved their lives yesterday from Usman Ali and his people and whom they had bade farewell early in the morning that same day.

"What the hell are you two doing there?" the soldier asked them, aiming his M14 rifle at them.

"There was an unconscious boy lying here, sir," Danny replied.

"Who is he?"

"We don't know, sir. There was also a man with a horse. He galloped away when he saw us coming. He must have brought the boy here. The boy was gagged and fettered when we found him, but we have set him free."

"Who is he?"

"Who, sir?" Danny inquired in confusion.

"The boy, damn you!"

"We don't know him, sir."

"And the man with the horse?"

"We don't know him either."

"You two are proper riddle to me. I've been following you the whole day. You came here purposely. You were hurrying to this place as if your future depended on it. Don't tell me that you have nothing to do with him or that this is the first time you've seen him. If you keep on lying to me, I'll teach you two a severe lesson. I'll cut off your tongues for you."

"We came here in search of water," Danny explained. "It's a coincidence that we found this boy as well as the river."

"Where were you hurrying to, young man?" the soldier addressed Samuel. "You were the one leading the way."

"I felt insecure in following the river or taking rest near it. I was afraid of falling once again in the hands of people who could do us harm. I persuaded Danny to abandon the river and head eastwards where our pursuers may not reach us."

"How long have you two known each other?"

"We met on the morning when the medical facility was bombed by the jet," Danny replied.

"Where did you meet exactly and why did you decide to travel in the wilderness alone?"

Danny told him the truth for the second time.

"I told you to go to Filtu, but you deliberately picked the wrong direction. Why?"

"That part of the region is where our pursuers lived and pastured. We were afraid of being captured."

"You're lying. You were following a premeditated direction and heading towards a set destination. What on earth is going on here?"

He removed his combat knife from its sheath with his left hand and pointed it at them.

"Tell the truth or face the consequences."

"We've told you the truth, sir. If this boy ever wakes up, he can testify to our innocence."

"All right, bring the boy down."

Samuel climbed down and stood at the foot of the rock, facing the soldier. Danny lifted the unconscious boy by holding him under his armpits and slid him onto Samuel's back. Samuel staggered at the weight of the boy but managed to carefully let the boy lie down at the feet of the soldier. The soldier studied the unconscious boy and the bruises in his arms.

"It's unusual for abductions to take place in this region. The evildoer must have come a long way. Did you have a rendezvous with the man? Tell the truth."

"No, sir, we've had no rendezvous with anyone," Samuel replied.

"You're lying!" he barked at Samuel. Then turning to Danny, he asked, "How could you decide to follow a complete stranger in the wilderness? How could you be so sure that this boy was harmless and had no scheme of his own? You said your father is a soldier. I don't believe your story."

"Samuel saved my life, sir. I was a dying boy when I met him. I escaped from home purposely because I was dying. Everybody said I was dying. The doctors said I was dying. So I didn't care to follow Samuel. But Samuel saved my life. He's a good person."

"How could he have saved your life?"

"It's hard to explain, sir," said Danny, not believing he was using such an expression. "But this much I can say, Samuel doesn't have ill-intentions."

"What were you suffering from, if you were dying?"

"I cannot tell, sir. Even the doctors were unable to determine my illness."

"Can we do something for the boy, sir?" Samuel intervened.

The soldier relaxed a bit.

"Is he still alive?"

"He was alive a while ago."

"Remove his clothes and take a step back."

Samuel did as he was told and retreated. The soldier returned his knife into its sheath and knelt down with one leg to examine the boy. He felt his pulse in his neck, examined both eyes, and searched for any sign of torture or abuse all over his body.

"He's alive, all right. Except the bruises, he seems to be intact. He's unconscious from shock, most probably." He confirmed after a short while.

He placed his rifle next to him, on his right side, and removed his backpack from his back and placed it next to him, on his left side, and extracted a first-aid box from the backpack.

"Do you think he'll wake up, sir?" Samuel asked him anxiously.

"How the devil can I tell? You're the magician's servant, you should tell me! Which direction did the abductor take?"

They told him.

"He must have seen us descending the hill, which is why he abandoned his plan and escaped." Danny explained.

"Why did someone do such a cruel thing to him?"

"How the devil should I know?" snapped the soldier. "Possibly, as a fulfilment of some accursed ritual or as retribution for someone. Assuming your account is correct."

He turned his attention to the boy and patted his cheeks with both hands gently.

"Can you hear me, young man?" he queried, but the boy did not make any reaction.

The soldier took out a plastic syringe, a small glass bottle containing glucose powder, and a minute plastic water bottle from his first-aid box. Using his syringe, he mixed the water with the glucose powder, shook the bottle gently, and injected the boy with the glucose.

"Go and fetch water from the river." He gave his water bottle to Samuel.

Samuel rushed to fetch water. When he returned, the soldier wetted a piece of cloth from his box and gently rubbed the boy's body with it.

"We have to wait and see how he responds to the injection. You should move him to the other side of the rock, in the shade." He stood up and addressed Danny: "Come down and assist your friend."

Danny came down. The boys moved the unconscious boy to the other side of the rock where there was some shade.

"Can I go to the hill and collect our belongings, sir? We left them there when we were having a break. We also left our water bottle there." Danny asked.

"You're not my captive, why do you ask my permission?"

"I'll be right back."

"The devil take you!"

But Danny headed to the river.

"Where the hell are you going?"

"I must get a drink. I'm absolutely parched."

Thinking the boy was now safe in the hands of the soldier, Samuel elected to accompany Danny but the soldier snapped at him.

"You stay right here! One is enough to collect the rags."

"I too am parched, sir."

"I don't care. Drink from my water bottle. You need to answer a few questions before I decide to let you go."

Samuel drank from the water bottle.

"Now back to you, young man," the soldier came closer to Samuel and stood in front of him. "You owe me an explanation. Think about your answer very carefully or else it'll cost you your tongue today."

"I've told you the truth all along, sir."

"I refuse to believe your story. Where are you from originally, where did your parents live? Why did you come to Dolo? Why did you decide to go to the wilderness instead of the military camp in Dolo?"

"I hardly know my parents, sir. I was raised by a prophet from childhood. The prophet never lived in one place and I moved with him from one place to another." Samuel stubbornly repeated his story.

"When was the last time you saw your parents?"

"A long time ago. I don't remember the time, sir. I'm not good in remembering dates and places."

"When was the last time you saw your priest?"

"Not long ago."

"When? Damn you!"

"Six Sundays ago."

"Where exactly was it?"

"We were in a small remote village, sir, where we celebrated Easter with the local people. It was there I last saw him."

"What's the town called?"

"You mean the village? I forgot what it's called. I don't have a good recollection of places, sir. We travelled a lot and constantly changed places. We rarely stayed in one place for so long."

"Why did you depart from the priest in the first place?"

"The prophet had an important journey to make and he wanted to travel alone."

"Where did he want to travel, I need a precise answer."

"It's called Mount Hor, sir."

"Where on earth is this mountain?"

"I cannot tell you, sir. He always referred to it as the Great Mountain, but he's never said where it's located."

"And you never asked him?"

"No, sir, I never asked him. He'd have told me had it been necessary."

"You're deliberately giving me foggy answers none of which makes sense. What the hell are you doing here in the wilderness?"

"I'm searching for the prophet."

"Why do you search for him if he's travelling."

"He should have been back a long time ago."

"Why didn't you go to the mountain where he went?"

"I don't know where it is, sir."

"But why here, why didn't you search for him elsewhere?"

"I've searched for him everywhere for many days, but in vain. One day I met some merchants who were just returning from Dolo. They maintained to have seen an old man travelling alone in the wilderness. From their description, I suspected that they might have seen the prophet. That's how I came to Dolo."

"Were they travelling along the Ganale River themselves? I've never heard of merchants travelling along the Ganale River. Were they travelling on foot?"

"They said they were contraband merchants, but I have no idea how they were travelling."

"And you believed them?"

"Why should I doubt them? Besides, their description was compelling."

"Where did you meet these merchants?"

"I met them in Neghelle. They were about to set off to Addis Ababa that same day."

"So you're telling me that in this vast and desolate place where you could have taken any direction and been completely lost, you just happened to pick the one right direction which brought you straight to this place to find an abundance of water and this boy lying on a rock?"

"We set the hill as our target, because it was the only target we could see from afar."

"Surely you knew that by abandoning the river you were heading towards your destruction. This doesn't make sense."

"I see your point, sir. Against all odds, I decided to follow an inner voice. I was right in following it."

"At first I thought you two were some common swindlers, but I now see that I was mistaken. Most likely you are informers and trying to pass some vital information to the enemy in the east. There must be a third person awaiting you somewhere. It's also very likely that you have something to do with the man who abducted this boy."

"To think of us as informers is absurd, sir."

"Nothing is absurd in times of war. The two-legged creatures are full of contradictions and capable of undertaking absurd and nasty things."

"But how would we profit by being informers, sir?"

"How the devil should I know? That's what I want to find out."

"No, sir, we're not informers. We work for no one. We were desperate to save our lives. But I now see that an invisible hand led us to this place."

"An invisible hand, indeed!"

"Why, sir, the people who tried to kill us yesterday might also think that your coming was no accident, that it was premeditated and that we worked for you. But we've never seen you before and certainly we don't work for you. Your coming might have been preordained, but it was not premeditated."

The soldier meditated on Samuel's response.

"You're hiding a great mystery from me, but this time I'll not rest until I've unraveled it."

Saying this, he took a few steps back and searched with his eyes for a shaded place to rest.

"So, you elect not to desert your friend, after all," the soldier remarked when Danny joined them.

"What do you mean, sir?"

"Never mind. Now young man, I'll give you another chance to explain who you are and what's going on here. Even if you admit that you are informers, I'm willing and ready to forgive you, considering how young and inexperienced you are. Perhaps, one of you, or even both of you, has some compelling reasons for your actions. Perhaps, someone has threatened to hurt your parents?"

This time Danny confessed everything.

"You're the son of Colonel Adam, the physician?" the soldier inquired unable to conceal his astonishment.

"I am, sir."

"When was the last time you saw your father?"

Danny told him.

"Do you know where he's now?"

"He's dead."

"I'm very sorry, son. Who else do you know in Dolo?"

"My sister was also in Dolo. She too is dead. She was a nurse."

This admission made a great difference, for now the soldier regarded Danny with great compassion.

"What on earth are you doing here in the wilderness, how do you know this boy?"

Danny fixed his eyes on the ground in silence. He was suddenly overcome by the memory of his father and Zema. The soldier went to him and stood next to him.

"I'm sorry about your father and sister. I knew your father personally. We've been together to many places in the east. A talented and industrious fellow he was. Always went after danger, though. He was a daredevil. He had a way with the ladies. He needn't have to come to Dolo, mind you. He could have stayed in Neghelle, instead. The army has lost a talented man."

Danny still kept silent, trying to suppress the sobs rising from his chest.

"You, too, seem to have taken after your father. Your coming to Dolo wasn't a wise idea, but worse was your decision to follow this stranger in the wilderness."

Chapter 22

They decided to spend the night by the river and set off to Filtu very early the next morning. The unconscious boy did not wake the entire day nor did he show any sign of improvement despite the fact that the soldier had given him another injection.

"If he doesn't wake up in the morning, we shall carry on without him," he told the boys.

"Leaving him here alone, sir?" Samuel screamed in shock.

"What else do you want to do with him? Bury him alive?"

"Why, sir, take him with us."

"How? Can you travel carrying him? I have no time to waste, I have some pressing assignments to carry out."

"Can't you leave without us, sir? Danny and I will take care of him. We can manage to survive for a few days by ourselves. Who knows, he might recover tomorrow and be able to walk on his own. If he dies, we shall give him a proper burial."

"I can't take care of him, he's not my responsibility. Besides, I'm fed up with this journey," Danny protested resignedly, avoiding eye contact with Samuel.

"In that case, please allow me to stay with him, sir. You take Danny with you. I assure you I'll be fine."

"Are you out of your mind?" Danny yelled at Samuel in frustration.

"You'll come with us," the soldier interfered curtly.

"How can we leave a dying boy alone, sir? Isn't that cowardly?"

The soldier was furious.

"Don't you dare tell me what's cowardice and what's gallantry, damn you!" he thundered. "I'm accustomed to making hard decisions in difficult times and this is not in the least bit difficult. You'll come with us. Besides, I don't trust you."

They were sitting next to the rock, gathered around a small fire and eating the last bits of grilled meat from the day before, which they warmed up by extending the meat over the fire using sticks. The unconscious boy, now tightly wrapped up in Samuel's jacket, was lying next to the fire. After they had finished eating, they collected the bones and buried them next to the rock. The boys were very tired and desperate to lie down and sleep. But in that instant, the boy's eyes suddenly opened and he appeared to stare blankly into the darkness. Samuel was the first to notice. He sprang to his feet and rushed to kneel down beside him.

"Hello," he greeted him cheerfully. "Can you hear me?"

The eyes blinked twice, but they were blurred and did not seem to register anything in particular. The soldier and Danny joined Samuel and knelt down beside him.

"Can you hear us, young man, what's your name?" the soldier asked him.

The boy reacted by shifting his gaze away from Samuel towards the soldier and from the soldier to Danny and back to Samuel again.

"Who are you, young man?" the soldier inquired once again.

"Do you understand us?" Danny asked him in Somali.

The boy blinked once feebly and closed his eyes.

"It's a good sign that he's opened his eyes. We must give him something to eat. One of you should lift him up gently," the soldier ordered.

While the boys lifted him up and supported him from behind, the soldier brought out a dry biscuit from his backpack, crushed it inside a metal cup, poured water into the cup, and, using his index finger, mixed the contents to make porridge.

"Now let's see how much of this he can take," he said.

The boy was uncooperative, but they prized open his mouth and poured the porridge into it, some of which he swallowed involuntarily. They also made him take some water.

"I think he's fine. But he's still in a state of shock and it's also likely that he wishes to stay in the same state."

"What do you mean, sir?" Danny ventured to ask him.

"What I mean is this. He doesn't know who we are and he may not speak Amharic. So, he may not be able to tell whether we are friends or enemies. Since he can't set himself free, one way to deny his agony is to perpetuate the state of shock."

"We should wake him up and reassure him that we're his friends, that we are there to help him and not to harm him."

"We can't wake him up. When I say he's decided to stay in the state of shock, I don't mean he's made the decision consciously. His mind may be in control of his decision, but the boy may not be in control of his mind. His unconscious mind is more likely in control."

"What must we do then?"

"We should wait. He can't remain unconscious indefinitely. But we should handle the situation very carefully, otherwise, he may lose his mind."
Despite the uncertainty of what lay ahead, all of them felt glad to have caught a glimpse of hope that the boy was coming back to life.

They all slept peacefully throughout the night. The soldier was the first to wake up. He got up and went to the river, did some exercises, and washed in the river. When he returned, the boys were still fast asleep. Seeing how exhausted and defenseless they looked in their sleep, he felt sorry for them for the first time. After all, the thought crossed his mind, these boys might be innocent. All the same, he was disconcerted, because he was unable to decide what to do with them and with the boy.
"It's time to get up," he shook them each in turn. Samuel woke up immediately and sat up. But Danny refused to be woken up.
"Get up, Danny," Samuel patted Danny on the shoulder gently.
"Let him sleep for a little longer. Perhaps, it's better if you and I talk in private. Now about this boy, what should be done?"

"I'm hoping that he'll show some sign of improvement over the course of the day."

"Suppose he does. What's next?"

Samuel stood up.

"We should give him some time to recover and then take him with us."

"Where?"

"If he regains consciousness, he'll tell us where he comes from. We can bring him to his family. I'm sure by now they're dying of worry."

"How about your own journey?"

"If the boy comes from one of the surrounding villages, why, sir, his parents may help us on our journey by way of gratitude. After all, we've saved the boy's life."

"Suppose he doesn't wake up; he doesn't recover from the shock?"

"That would be very unfortunate, but we must do everything we can to help him recover."

"I can't stay here any longer. I'm on a special mission and have to report to my regiment. I've already wasted two precious days on account of you."

"I understand, sir. Take Danny with you, but allow me to stay with the boy."

"Listen, boy, I can see how stubborn you are. You're making an injudicious and dangerous proposal. Leaving you alone with this boy means letting him and you perish at the same time. You cannot take care of him and yourself at the same time. I can't allow this to happen in all good conscience. Besides, Danny will be very upset, for I've observed his attachment to you."

"But I can't leave the boy behind. I'll not forgive myself if I do that. Eventually, Danny, too, will come to his senses and blame himself for deserting a helpless boy. He has a delicate conscience, I'm sure of this."

The soldier unfurled his arms with an air of frustration.

"My choices are limited. I must report to my superiors today. I took a liberty yesterday in following you. You'll come with us, young man. This much is a done deal. The best we can do for this boy is to feed him and to make him lie down under the rock where there'll be plenty of shade. We can leave a few dry biscuits and your water bottle beside him. As soon as we come to the next village, and I'm sure we shall come across one before the end of the day, we shall inform them of his whereabouts and explain his situation. They'll come and rescue him."

"Suppose they refuse to rescue him?"

"His case falls under a collective responsibility. They'll rescue him because it's an order. Otherwise, there'll be consequences. The villagers understand very well that we're in a war."

"Suppose we fail to find a village nearby? What'll happen to him?"

"We shall find a village nearby, that's for sure, and the villagers will not refuse to rescue him. I'm sure this boy belongs to one of their clans."

"Suppose he gets up in the meantime and wanders off aimlessly in the wilderness?"

"He won't go too far, will he? In his condition, he's bound to stay around. A rescue team will find him."

"Suppose some wild animals find him?"

"Damn you! You are not permitted to interrogate me!"

"With all due respect, sir, I can't come with you. Please, don't force me to come with you. Let me stay with him."

Meanwhile, Danny got up and stood beside Samuel.

"Come with us, Samuel, please!" he begged him.

"I can't come with you. I must stay with him."

The soldier set his arms akimbo with palpable vexation and stared fixedly at Samuel. He deliberated for a brief moment.

"Damn, damn, damn!" he cursed. "Very well, then. You two will take turns to carry the boy. We'll see how far we can trudge like this."

This proposal pleased Samuel, but Danny unfurled his arms with great frustration and turned his back on both the soldier and Samuel.

"I'll carry the boy," Samuel was quick to reassure Danny. "I'm sure the boy is not heavy, considering the great ordeal he has endured."

"You'll not be able to support yourself let alone another burden. But we shall see. Now, don't stand there and stare at me. We have a lot to get done before we set off. We have to feed him and give him a glucose injection and search for some food for ourselves. Get to work!"

Saying this, he knelt down beside the boy to examine him. The boy was already awake.

"Good morning," he greeted him, slightly taken aback.

The boy did not answer him. His eyes looked terrified. Danny and Samuel knelt down, one on either side of the soldier and looked at him with compassion.

"How are you feeling?" Danny asked him in Somali forgetting his grave disconcertment just a while ago.

"Who are you?" whispered the boy in Somali with a tremulous and hoarse voice.

"We came here yesterday by accident and found you lying on a rock, unconscious. You were fettered and gagged. Can you tell us what happened?"

The boy did not answer him, but his eyes were filled with tears.

"What's your name?" the soldier asked him in Somali.

"Abdelkadir," the boy managed to answer.

"Translate for me, will you?" the soldier turned to Danny. Then, turning to Abdelkadir, he asked, "How did you come here, do you remember?"

The boy barely nodded his head.

"Is this the first time you've seen these boys?" the soldier asked the boy in Somali.

The boy looked at him in bewilderment.

"What's the last thing you can remember?"

The boy stared at the soldier blankly.

"Are you able to get up?"

The soldier extended his hand and helped him to sit up.

"Give him water to drink," he ordered Samuel.

"Here, drink!" Samuel urged him, passing his water bottle to the boy.

The boy accepted, but after taking one mouthful, he immediately spat the water out, wincing in disgust.

"Your taste buds are bitter," the soldier told him, "You haven't eaten or drunk properly for some time. Rinse your mouth out with water, it may get better."

The boy rinsed his mouth twice with water. Then he tried to drink but could not. He spat the water out and returned the water bottle to Samuel, closing his eyes tightly once again.

"You must drink, young man. Give him the bottle."

The boy obeyed.

"Where are you from young man, where does your family live?"

"I'm from the village of Ali Fander."

"Who's your father?"

"Abdul Wahad Abdo."

"Is your father a prominent man in his clan?"

The boy nodded his head in agreement.

"How far is your village from the River Ganale?"

"The village is not directly on the River Ganale, but it's not very far from it. My village stands on top of a hill and can be seen from a distance. It has six water wells of its own from which we and our animals drink every day."

"Do you remember who brought you here?"

"Where am I?"

"I'm afraid you're very likely very far from home."

The boy shook his head and closed his eyes. He looked exhausted.

"Shouldn't we let him rest a little?" Samuel intervened.

"Now, we'll give you breakfast, young man, and try to feed you, but you must help us. You should also take some more water, for your body has lost a considerable amount of fluid. Afterwards, I'll give you an injection. It's only glucose. Then we shall let you rest."

This time the boy cooperated. After breakfast, he was given an injection and thereafter he fell asleep immediately.

Chapter 23

The three ate the soldier's last slices of black bread and when they had finished, Samuel went to the river to try his luck in fishing even though the river was shallow. The soldier, on the other hand, preferred to try bird hunting. Danny bathed in the river and then came back and lay down next to Abdelkadir.

After twenty minutes or so, Samuel came running.

"Danny get up!" he urged.

"What's the matter, what happened?"

"Come, hurry, I want to show you something?"

"Is it something terrible?"

"Come, come, we've no time."

Samuel ran back with all his might and Danny followed him. After they had run for a few minutes, Samuel stopped next to the river bank where a modest acacia tree was standing.

"Do you see here?"

"What do I see?" Danny took a cursory look at and around the tree but he could not spot anything.

"Just look carefully, next to the tree, please, will you? What do you see?"

"I don't see anything."

"Why, here!" Samuel went to the tree and pointed at a small hole in the ground.

"I see a hole. What can it be?"

"Why, someone must have uprooted a plant, a tree."

"Someone must have been here already; is that what you mean? It must be the soldier, if it wasn't you."

"It wasn't I and the soldier hasn't been to this place. I came here by myself."

"Who do you think must have done that? The boy's abductor?"

"I doubt it."

"Then, who else?"

Samuel did not reply.

"Why should we care?" Danny asked impatiently.

"You're right, we shouldn't care at all. Come, we must go back."

When they returned, they met the soldier who asked them where they had been.

"We were looking at something," Samuel replied dismissively.

"Did you get anything to eat?"

"Unfortunately, no, we didn't get anything to eat."

The soldier, too, had returned empty-handed.

"We must set off now," the soldier ordered. "This place has no food to offer. We should try to reach Ganale as quickly as we can."

They set off around eight o'clock in the morning. Samuel used his jacket to carry the boy on his back. To Samuel's great surprise and dismay, the boy was heavy.

"Why is your backpack so heavy, sir?" Danny ventured to ask the soldier.

The soldier was about to snap at Danny but then he changed his mind.

"Because it has an old radio in it."

"A radio?" Danny shouted in surprise.

"Don't get so excited," the soldier checked him coolly. "It's more dead than alive."

"Isn't it possible to send a radio message to Neghelle or Filtu?"

"Theoretically, it should transmit within a radius of 70 kilometers. But, as I said, the radio is very old and establishes connection only when it pleases. Its battery is not in an excellent condition, to begin with. When I was on the other side of the Ganale River, I was able to establish a connection. Yesterday, however, as I was following you on this side of the river, I wasn't successful."

"What's your mission in the wilderness, sir? I'm sure this radio is a precious device to carry around in the wilderness."

"It's none of your business. Don't ask stupid questions."

They travelled in silence, but the soldier relented once again.

"I monitor the movements of enemy agents in this region. Some agents are more dangerous than a whole regiment. We share a long border with the enemy. Agents can very easily infiltrate our border."

Nothing else was said thereafter. They travelled for about two hours with several short breaks in between, because Samuel was very tired. Then they decided to take a long rest. Abdelkadir was by then already awake.

"How are you feeling?" the soldier asked him while Samuel carefully placed him down on the ground and collapsed on the ground next to Abdelkadir. Abdelkadir gave no answer. They gave him water to drink and waited. When no response was forthcoming, the soldier cleared his voice and put in his next question and Danny translated for him.

"Do you know the man who abducted you?"

"I don't know him," he answered with a melancholy tone.

"Do you remember how he abducted you?"

Abdelkadir did not answer immediately but he answered in the affirmative at length.

"I was abducted when I was tending the camels. My father has six camels."

"What time was it when he abducted you?"

"I was just returning from lunch."

"Tell us what exactly happened."

"The man came from behind and clutched me in his strong arms. I tried to free myself and bit his hand with all my strength, but he was too strong for me. He threw me on the ground forcefully and held a big knife to my throat."

"Was he alone?"

"Yes, he was alone."

"Was he armed, did he have a rifle?"

"I don't know if he had a rifle. But as I said, he had a big knife."

"What did he look like?"

"He had a big, muscular body. His head was completely shaven. His upper body was bare and his upper arms and head were covered with big scars."

"What was he wearing?"

"He was wearing a macawis."

"Did he say why he was abducting you?"

"No."

"Was he a Somali?"

"I don't think he was a Somali. He didn't utter a single word, though. But by the look of him, I could tell that he wasn't a Somali. Somalis are lean and tall, but this man was stout and short."

"What happened next?"

The boy's eyes suddenly became fiery, his face turned pale, and his lips began to tremble.

"I have no wish to distress you, my boy," the soldier tried to soothe him. "In order to find and punish this man, it's important to have an accurate account of what's happened."

"After he threw me on the ground," Abdelkadir went on in trembling voice, tears now blurring his vision, "he inserted a disgusting rag in my mouth and gagged me with another piece of cloth. I felt very sick from the taste and smell of the rag inside my mouth. He tied my hands together with a rope and slung me across a mule. The mule wasn't saddled for a ride, but a thick blanket and a leather mat were placed on its back. He jumped on behind me and tied me to himself and he galloped away. I tried to concentrate but I was unable to. I was very sick."

"Did you travel all the way to the river, without stopping?"

"I suppose we travelled the whole afternoon and a long time in the dark. I thought I could hear the laughter of hyenas. Finally, he stopped and dismounted the mule and lifted me down. He tied the mule and me to a tree or a bush and we spent the night there."
"Did he give you something to eat?" Danny asked naively.
"No."
"Were you able to sleep?"
"I couldn't sleep for a long time. I was very sick and exhausted and it was very cold. Then I had terrible dreams."
"When did you set off again?"
"It must have been very early in the morning, before sunrise."
"He didn't say anything to you all this time?"
"Not a word."
"Do you have any suspicions as to why he tried to harm you?"
Tears rolled down the boy's cheeks. He half-closed his eyes and shook his head in sadness.
"Try to think carefully. Are you sure you haven't seen the man before? Have you heard your father or any of the member of your village speak of this person? Perhaps he had some quarrel with your father?"
Abdelkadir shook his head in the negative.

"I've never seen him before."

"Was your village in some disagreement or quarrel with another village, which might have wished to take revenge?"

"I don't think so."

"Maybe there was a quarrel because of the water wells?"

The boy sank into deep melancholy, closed his eyes completely, and refused to answer.

"Was there?"

"Not that I know of."

"We should let him rest a little," Samuel intervened.

"Has he done something nasty to me?" Abdelkadir asked, his face suddenly turning pale. From the palpable horror displayed in his eyes it was evident that he was expecting an affirmative, shocking answer.

"If I understand your meaning correctly, no, I don't think he's done anything nasty to you. The boys arrived just in time to save you."

Abdelkadir removed the jacket which was wrapped around him and felt his penis with his right hand.

"Do you think he was trying to castrate you?" the soldier asked him.

Abdelkadir did not reply him. His entire body suddenly trembled.

"We must let him rest," Samuel insisted.

The soldier consented. While the boys rested, he removed a small notebook from his backpack and wrote down the substance of his conversation with Abdelkadir. After they had rested for about half an hour, they were ready to set off once again.

"Do you think you can walk by yourself?" the soldier asked Abdelkadir.

"I can try."

He was not ready to walk. His legs wobbled and he was about to collapse, but the soldier reacted quickly and took him in his arms. Danny offered to carry Abdelkadir, but Samuel declined the offer, suggesting that Abdelkadir was his responsibility.

Chapter 24

The soldier was very anxious to reach the river, so that he could establish contact with his base that day. Samuel too was eager to arrive at the river, where he hoped to catch fish for supper. However, they could not travel as fast as they had wished. They trudged through the wilderness instead, as the soldier had anticipated and feared, for the sun was too strong, the heat was unbearable, and Samuel was sweating a lot. Yet all of them restrained themselves, as far as they could, from consuming too much water, because they wanted to keep the water for Abdelkadir. Around two o'clock they arrived at a place where there were some red rocks and dwarf cactus plants. The soldier decided to take a rest there.

"We shall resume our journey late in the afternoon. I'm exhausted and so are you."

The boys consented instantly. The soldier found fragments of dry biscuits in his backpack and gave some of them to the boys. The rest he diluted with water and fed Abdelkadir. He himself cut cactus pads with his knife, removed the thorns, peeled the crust, and cut the pads to pieces and began to eat.

"Isn't it poisonous?" Danny asked him.

"No. I used to survive on this diet alone for days when I was in Ogaden. It's nutritious and rich in water. If you don't wish to swallow the fibrous part, you can chew the pad, swallow the water, and spit the rest out."

"You've been stationed in Ogaden?"

"Yes, I have. I trained there as a Special Airborne Commando after I'd left the Harar Military Academy."

"My father was in Ogaden."

"Yes, I know."

"Can I try it?"

"Please."

Danny took a piece into his mouth and chewed it cautiously. But he spat it out immediately.

"I don't like it."

"If it's not poisonous," Samuel said coming forward, "I'll eat it. Can I have some, please?"

The soldier gave him a piece.

"I don't care how it tastes, as long as it quenches my thirst and stills my hunger."

Samuel chewed and swallowed one piece after another.

"You are adept, you'll have no problem surviving in the wilderness," the soldier remarked.

"Well, I've eaten a snake. He's also eaten a snake."

"You astonish me. When was that?"

They told him.

"Nature can supply you with enough nourishment if you're willing to put aside your prejudices."

"Let me try another piece."

Danny made up his mind to eat another piece and then another.

"I've this funny feeling, though, that I'm about to throw up."

"It's a normal reaction. You're acting against your mind. Your mind is the problem, not the cactus."

"Aren't you afraid when you travel alone in the wilderness?" Danny asked the soldier.

"I'm always cautious. As a combat soldier I live with an abiding awareness of imminent danger. So, I can't afford to be heedless. But I'm not particularly afraid because I'm alone."

"How many people have you killed so far?"

"Never ask a soldier such a question. A good soldier never kills a fly unless he has to. If he must kill, however, the number of enemy casualties is not his immediate concern. If he sees one of his comrades in harm's way, he'll kill thousands of enemy soldiers, if he must, in order to rescue his comrade."

"Were you testing me this morning when you suggested leaving Abdelkadir behind?" Samuel asked the soldier.

"What makes you ask this question?"

"I was just wondering."

"I once was passing a church by and saw a beautiful bird landing in front of the entrance gate," Danny intervened presently. "I threw a stone I was holding in my hand and killed the bird. I didn't know why I threw the stone. I was very sorry for the bird afterwards and couldn't forget it for a long time."

"You've raised an interesting subject," the soldier remarked. "I've been thinking a lot about human nature lately. This is one of the curses, or the gifts, if you will, of spending too much time in the wilderness alone. Thinking too much, I mean. So, I don't mind sharing my ideas with you. I'm sure you two are mature enough to understand me. Let me begin by asking you a question. Imagine two complete strangers meeting in a desolate place where there is no witness. Both men or women or a man and a woman, it doesn't matter who they are. Let's assume that none of them has any conflict of interest and none of them is interested in the service or property of the other. Let's say they are fully content with their lives. So, there is no sexual, financial, labor, or any other advantage coming into question. Now, imagine one of them is fully armed whereas the other is not. What do you think will ensue as a result of their encounter?"

The boys looked at the soldier with a look of confusion. At last Samuel reacted.

"Since you've assumed that the two are disinterested in one another, nothing should transpire. The two will go their separate ways."

"But I have said that one of them is armed whereas the other isn't."

"I don't see the relevance of this revelation."

"The armed will kill the unarmed?" Dawit answered, counting his words.

"Why should you say so?" the soldier asked with an animated voice.

"I don't know. The armed man may say the devil induced him to kill him."

"This is outrageous," Samuel protested.

"It is not," the soldier countered, fixing his eyes on Danny. "Why should he kill a man who hasn't done him anything?"

"I firmly believe that the armed man will kill the unarmed man. That's how it will end. That's how it's bound to end," the soldier insisted.

"But why?"

"Because of the gun he carries."

"I don't get it. Do you mean the gun has a will of its own? The man may kill to defend his interest or in case he is frightened. But I don't think he kills aimlessly."

"The fact that human beings exploit the defenselessness and ignorance of their neighbors to their own advantage doesn't need any proof. In fact, some of the famous philosophers have already claimed that it's in the nature of human instincts to be aggressive. But my claim goes beyond all this."

"What's your claim then?" Danny asked.

"You see, the problem is with human freedom. The gun, the absence of any consequences, the defenselessness of the other person, all, give the armed man infinite freedom. Human beings cannot abide it when a slice of their freedom is removed, neither can they abide infinite freedom."

"This is hard to accept," Samuel remarked.

The soldier looked at the boys alternately, undecided, palpably struggling with himself.

"This is something I have proved practically. I could tell you stories after stories to ascertain my claim. Stories you'd never believe. Stories..."

The soldier left his sentence hanging in mid-air.

"What stories, sir?" Danny asked him almost inaudibly.

"No, no, no," the soldier shook his head, "they had better remain untold..."

"Come on, sir, tell us at least one of them," Danny ventured to say.

"No, no, they are too hot to handle. Suffice to say, I knew a person of prominent standing who had done someone in, if you know what I mean. Unprovoked. The person himself confessed it to me on his deathbed, long after I had developed my theory, mind you, and without ever being aware of my theory. Human beings cannot abide infinite freedom, believe me."

There was an awkward silence for a while and then the soldier spoke once again.

"But when I say this, I don't mean, of course, you killed the bird because of the superiority of your position. On second thoughts, though, who knows, perhaps you killed it because of the superiority of your position, after all.

Philosophy aside," the soldier suddenly softened his tone and continued, gently tapping the ground with the butt of his rifle, "sometimes the memory of a seemingly insignificant incidents lingers in the mind for a long time. When I was in the ninth grade, I fell in love with the girl who was sitting next to me. She was very shy but very good at school. I myself wasn't amongst the bravest where girls were concerned, but I guess she knew my feelings for her. She was always kind to me. But one day, during a break, unbeknown to me I sat on a dirty bench and the dirt left its mark on my trousers at the back. When I returned to the class, I decided to scribble something on the blackboard, something I had never done before. Suddenly, I heard a giggle from behind and looked back. It was the girl and her friend who were giggling, pointing at my trousers. I looked at my trousers but couldn't spot the dirt. Normally I wouldn't pay much attention to girls giggling but that day it somehow annoyed me very much. I went straight to her and gave her a slap in the face in front of the whole class. Whatever induced me to do so I couldn't tell, then or even now. I regretted my action instantly, but was too proud to apologize. She left the class in embarrassment, but she didn't report me to the principal. I apologized to her the next day and she accepted my apology. Nonetheless, it took me a long time to forgive myself. Even now I remember the incident with embarrassment."

"Did you confess your love to her eventually?" Danny asked him.

"Unfortunately, no. After my misconduct, harnessing the courage became impossible for me. Two months later the school closed for the summer break and she and her family moved to a different city. Her father was a police officer. I never saw her again."

"You never tried to search for her afterwards?"

"I never tried. My means were limited, really, I came from a poor family. When I finished high school I joined the military academy and from then on my life has been very busy."

"Are you married now, sir?"

"Yes, I am. I have three children, a boy and two girls."

"The prophet used to say that self-forgiveness is a show of great confidence in the capacity of the person we have wronged to forgive us completely," Samuel said.

"In my case, the bird couldn't forgive me. It could never be the same again." Danny asserted sorrowfully.

"But God can. The bird belonged to God. As far as God is concerned, everything can be recovered if we confess our sin."

Silence ensued. Both the soldier and Danny were thinking about Abdelkadir and his abductor. In the light of the ordeal he had undergone, they could not imagine that one day Abdelkadir would be willing and able to forgive his abductor. Indeed, the thought of forgiveness in general appeared to them as a difficult hurdle to surmount.

"There is an inherent nastiness in all of us," the soldier broke the silence. "When I grew up, I was determined not to be like my father, not to repeat the mistakes he had made as a father, a husband, and a fellow human being. I thought I'd be generous, understanding, and forgiving. But whenever I go home and I'm with my wife and children I can't help noticing how disorganized, undisciplined, and passive they can be. Then, against my best judgement, I say and do nasty things. When I stand in front of the mirror, I see the image of my father, his piercing, critical, and disapproving eyes, and I recoil from it. So, I prefer to retreat to the battlefields. It seems to me being a soldier is the only thing I do well. It's impossible to exist without forgiveness, though. Samuel has made a point."

This was the first time the soldier addressed Samuel by his name.

"Wasn't there ever a time when you regretted being a soldier?" Danny asked him.

"Oh, there were times. Many times, indeed. But it's all right to regret, I think. Regret is like physical pain, unpleasant but useful."

"Why did you regret it?"

"As a soldier, I must obey orders from my superiors whether or not I agree with them. Regrettably, the leaders from whom the orders emanate are not the best trees our country has grown. If the mind is bad, its ideas are inevitably bad. Often times I was obliged to execute orders which destroyed the lives of hundreds of people."

"When my father was at the university, some generals tried to overthrow the emperor. They were all killed."

"A decade later other soldiers succeeded. Now look where we are."

"Would it have been better had they not overthrown the emperor?"

"Sometimes in life the distinction between good and bad is not at all unambiguous. The choice, likewise, is not between good and bad. Sometimes, one is forced to choose between two equally bad choices. The previous regime was bad but the current is worse. Admittedly, we may not have all the knowledge or the insight we need to make the right decision."

"What are your other regrets?"

"Why are you so interested to know about my regrets, young man?"
"It's good to know that others too have regrets. I have many of them."
"When my kids were very young, I should have spent more time with them. You can't expect people to follow your example when they hardly know you. If you want to influence people, you need to establish a relationship with them first. But enough about my regrets."

Chapter 25

From where they had taken their rest to the river was only a short distance. It was still daylight when they arrived at the river. Samuel and Danny swam cross the river, but the soldier spent some time testing the depth of the river with Samuel's staff, for he had to cross the river on foot in order to transport his backpack and Abdelkadir. After they had all crossed, they occupied themselves with different activities. The soldier moved from place to place trying to establish contact with his base. Samuel went fishing and Danny went collecting twigs. They let Abdelkadir rest in a shaded place near the river where Samuel was fishing. It was still hot and the air was stagnant.

Suddenly Danny came running to the soldier.

"I saw some huts," he told him, gasping for air.

"Where did you see them?"

"Over there," he pointed towards north-west.

"How many huts exactly?"

"I didn't count them. But there are more than three or four."

The soldier stood up and collected his rifle.

"Come, let's go and see."

The two followed in the direction from where Danny had come and saw from a distance four poorly-built mud huts standing next to each other.

"Shall we go to them, sir? They may give us something to eat," Danny asked with some impatience.

"We must study our surroundings first. We should wait until it's dark."

"Should we go into hiding then?"

"Hiding won't be necessary. If someone finds us here, we shall explain what we're doing. We must always keep an eye on each other."

"Suppose they decide to attack us?"

"We can defend ourselves. But why should they attack us?"

"Why should Usman Ali and his men have try to attack us?"

"Because they were suspicious of you."

"Well, they'll be suspicious of us now."

"We shall see. Don't be alarmed. Stay in one place."

"Do you think they have some goats or camels?"

"Why? Do you plan to steal one?"

"Oh, no, sir. They may give us some milk to drink, that's all."

"Most of the people in the wilderness are not rich. You must also remember that it's a time of war."

"So, what shall we do?"

"We shall wait until it's dark and go to one of the huts. It's enough if they let us sleep under their roof."

"What about food? I'm dying of hunger."

"We shall see. Go and collect twigs. How's Samuel doing?"

"I'll go and see."

The soldier returned to the place where he had been testing his radio and Danny went to Samuel. Samuel had not caught a single fish and was on the brink of giving up.

"We saw some huts," Danny announced.

"Where? Is anyone living in them?"

"Over there. We don't know yet if there's anyone living there."

"What do you mean?"

"We only saw them from a distance. The soldier said we should wait until it's dark before we go and see."

"Go and study carefully. We need something to eat urgently. If people live in those huts, they may feed us. You and Abdelkadir can talk to them."

"Should I abandon collecting twigs?"

"Can't you do both tasks at the same time?"

"Suppose someone captures me?"

"Then shout for help. What did the soldier say we should do?"

"He said we should mind our own business for now."

"He's right. Then collect twigs while keeping a lookout. But don't go too far."

"Do we really need the twigs?"

"Perhaps not. But we need urgently something to eat."

"I'll go and study."

Danny abandoned collecting twigs and approached the huts as closely and as seamlessly as he could. Indeed, people were living in the huts. He saw some people sitting next to one of the huts -- two women, a child and a man. One of the women was very young, possibly the mother of the child, whereas the other was an elderly woman. The man was in his late twenties or early thirties, possibly the husband of the young woman and the father of the child. The child was not older than two years. The young woman was grinding something on a grinding stone and the elderly woman and the man were chatting. But soon the young woman finished her task and went inside with the child and shortly thereafter the rest followed them.

It was now getting dark and Danny felt very hungry and weak. As he was thinking of returning to the soldier, the soldier himself came.

"What did you observe?" he asked.

Danny told him.

"This is what we'll do. The three of you will stay behind. You must stay together. I'll go to the people and talk to them. I will take my gun but leave the radio behind. If everything is fine, I'll come back to you. If, on the other hand, something goes wrong, if, for example, you hear gunshots, don't rush to come to my aid. Watch and wait carefully. Give me fifteen, twenty minutes. If I'm not back by then, you should escape without me. Do not linger. Do you know how to operate a military radio?"

"No sir."

The soldier explained how to tune and fine-tune channels, adjust the height and orientation of the antenna, adjust the gain of the amplifier, and control the volume for a better signal quality.

"Take the radio with you as far as you can and try to reach and inform someone of what's happened. I've already tuned the radio to the appropriate channel. You see the letter A where the switch indicates? That's the appropriate channel. If you cannot pick up a signal on A, turn the switch to B, C, or D. Try different positions for a better signal quality. If you pick up a signal, press this button and speak into the microphone. Don't release the button while speaking. Begin a request by speaking: URGENT, BLACK LION speaking. Repeat these words until someone responds. You need three passwords in order to communicate, in the following order: BLACK LION, BLUE NILE, and BLACK FALCON. If and when someone responds, he'll ask you to confirm your identity. You'll answer BLACK LION. Then he'll ask you to state your regiment. This time you'll answer BLUE NILE. Finally, he'll ask you to state your mission. You'll answer BLACK FALCON. Remember the order. BLACK LION, BLUE NILE, and BLACK FALCON. Two blacks and a blue in between. A river between two animals. Then he should respond with the following confirmation: PEREGRINATION. Repeat this word."

Danny repeated it.

"Good. If he fails to confirm with this password, don't speak to him. Change the channel and try again. If everything goes well, he'll ask you to state your message. You'll tell him briefly who you are and what you have witnessed. Keep your message short. He may ask you to transmit the same message from three different places.

That means he wants to determine your approximate location. You'll always count one hundred steps before you make the next transmission. If the battery is dead, there is a reserve battery in the backpack. If you must leave the radio behind, break it to pieces before you go or throw it into the river. Don't leave it behind intact. Travel westwards, as I told you, to Filtu."

"Let me go with you, sir. I'll help you with the translation."

"I've thought about that. But if we meet a hostile group, no one will protect the others. That's why I think you should stay behind. Samuel has refused to use a rifle. Moreover, if the radio falls into the hands of the enemy, it can cause great damage. All of you should stay together."

"Have you managed to establish contact, sir?"

"I haven't. If everything is all right, I'll try later. Signal transmission is better at night."

"Can't I go with you, sir? The people may misunderstand you because of the language barrier. Or take Abdelkadir with you."

"Funny you should say that. I was sent to this region on a mission because I can speak their language."

"Well sir?"

"No, it's better if I go alone. I can defend myself better if I'm alone. Come now, we should go to the others."

Chapter 26

Samuel was sitting despondent next to Abdelkadir when they came to him. Abdelkadir was fast asleep. The soldier woke Abdelkadir and informed them of his plan. They followed him halfway and stayed behind. From there to the huts was about three hundred meters.

The soldier cautiously approached the huts in the dark and stopped about ten meters away from them.

"Aselam aleykum," he shouted twice.

There was no response. He waited for a moment and called out one more time. This time someone came out holding a small lamp. It was the young woman, carrying the child in the other arm. She stood terrified when she saw the shadow of the soldier, but he was quick to reassure her.

"Don't be afraid, I come in peace."

"Who's there?" A man came from behind and stood in front of the woman.

"Who are you and what do you want?" he asked the soldier with an unfriendly tone.

"I'm a soldier on a mission. I've been travelling the whole day and I've run out of food and drink. Besides which, I'm very exhausted. Can you receive me as your guest? I'll pay you for your hospitality. I've some money with me."

"Sorry, we don't have room."

"I can sleep on the bare floor."

"Just wait, please."

The man went to the next hut and after some minutes came back with an elderly man.

"Selam aleykum," the elderly man greeted the soldier.

"Aleykum selam."

"What do you want, soldier?" he asked him in Amharic.

The soldier repeated in Amharic what he had told the young man.

"How do we know that you are really a soldier and that you are here with peaceful intentions?"

"Other than my word of honor, I cannot show you any evidence."

"But anybody can claim that he is a soldier. These are difficult times, sir."

"I understand. But I'm a soldier. You can see from my weapon and my uniform."

"Give us a second, please."

The two men entered into the hut to have a private discussion and returned a short time later.

"We cannot determine whether you are here with peaceful intentions, sir. We also see that we don't have much choice, as it stands, since you are armed," the old man told the soldier after the discussion.

"Your suspicion is justified, old man. I'd have acted in the same way had I been standing in your shoes. But tonight I need your hospitality. I'm not asking this for my sake only, but also for the sake of some helpless boys."

"Who are these helpless boys and where are they?"

"I'll be right back. Just give me a few minutes. We shall explain everything to you."

The soldier left the two men standing and disappeared into the darkness, deciding to bring the boys and his radio with him. When he and the boys returned, there were already three men and the two women standing in front of the hut. The third man had a flashlight in his hand.

"Selam aleykum," Abdelkadir greeted the men.

"Aleykum selam," they replied.

Abdelkadir explained who he was and why they were there. The old man happened to know his father and the inhabitants of Ali Fander. He asked him several questions to determine that the boy had not been kidnapped by the soldier.

"We will not turn you away, soldier. You and the boys are kindly invited to be our guests," the old man said at long last, "Even though we cannot be certain of the purpose of this visit, we put our trust in Allah."

They were admitted into the hut, which was spacious and empty looking. There was no table or chair nor any other furniture. The floor was covered with clean, comfortable, and colorful carpets, adorned with many cushions. The crack-filled mud walls were bare except for a solitary picture which was hanging in the middle of the wall adjacent to the front door. It was the picture of a young man in a uniform.

"Oh," exclaimed the soldier, enraptured, "who's this young man?"

"He is my son." The old man approached the soldier and stood next to him, gazing at the picture.

"Where's he now?"

"In Ogaden, fighting for his country," replied the proud father.

"You have my greatest respect, old man, for being the father of a hero."

"Thank you." The old man bowed slightly with apparent satisfaction.

"And you yourself are a hero for proudly displaying the picture of a soldier in your hut in these uncertain times." The boys could not see the soldier's face but were almost sure that there were tears in his eyes. The young lady brought out a plastic bowl and water jug for them to wash their feet. They went outside once again and washed their feet, first the soldier, then Samuel, then Danny, and at last Abdelkadir. When they were finished, they went inside and sat on the carpets.

"How old is your son?" the soldier asked the old man.

"He's three years younger than Abdo," he indicated towards the young man standing next to the old woman. "Abdo is twenty-eight. He is my first-born. Dounya is his wife."

"How long have you been living here?"

"Not too long. I had a business and a house in Dolo but had to abandon both because of the war. Abdo and his wife moved to this place some months before us to cultivate maize and sorghum. Abdo has a sensitive mind, if you know what I mean, which prevented him from serving in the military or undertaking big responsibilities."

"Is the little boy his son?"

"Yes. He's two years old."

"And your younger son, is he married?"

"No, he isn't married yet. He said he would marry after the war."

"Is the old woman your wife?"

"That's right. And he," he pointed to the third man, "is my brother-in-law. His wife died recently. He is living with us. He, too, has a sensitive mind. He doesn't work and has no one to support him."

"Is it peaceful here?"

"So far yes, Alhamdulillah."

The young woman served tea with milk to the guests.

"Where do you get milk?" the soldier asked her. The young woman smiled shyly and left.

"She is very shy," the old man stepped in. "We breed some goats. Two of the does recently gave birth."

"It's interesting to see that life thrives in this part of the world."

"Man has great capacity to thrive, but war comes along and destroys everything."

"You have spoken wisely," the soldier commended him.

The boys were very tired and desperate both to eat something and sleep.

"We will give you something to eat boys, take heart," the old man encouraged them.

"Do you happen to have a radio?" the soldier asked him.

"We have but the batteries are dead. Besides, the signal is very weak here."

"Any news?"

"There was a heavy battle in Aboker Muti yesterday evening, but our soldiers were able to secure Harar and its environs. At the southern front, the enemy could not break through."

"This is good news."

"But it comes at a high price." The old man sighed painfully.

"The war will be over soon and everything will be all right. Your son will be back, take heart."

"In-sha Allah."

Meanwhile, the young woman served freshly baked chapatis which were devoured almost instantly. Subsequently, she brought a second round and thereafter a third round. After they had eaten, the boys went to sleep. The young couple and their son moved to the other hut, taking the old lady and her brother with them. The soldier, even though they were all very tired, decided to chat with the old man a little longer. He was intending to try the radio later that evening.

In the middle of the night Samuel woke Danny.

"What's up?" Danny whimpered without opening his eyes. He was unable to open his eyes.

"The soldier will leave us soon. He's managed to establish connection with his base."

"That's good news, I mean his establishing connection."

"I'm sure he's told them about you."

"Possibly."

"Your poor mother will rejoice when she learns that you're still alive. They'll definitely break the news to her tomorrow."

"I'm not so sure."

"You're not sure about what?"

"Can I go back to sleep? Please."

"Up to now she has probably been thinking that you died in the bomb attack."

"It doesn't matter what she believed about me."

"Don't be hard on her."

"I'm not."

"Listen," Samuel whispered, but Danny was not listening. He was asleep.

After an hour or so, Samuel woke Danny for the second time.

"Oh, Samuel, what's wrong with you!" He protested vehemently. "What is it you want to talk about? Can't it wait till morning? I'm very tired."

"The prophet is dead," Samuel told him with a broken heart.

Danny forced himself to listen.

"How do you know?"

"I've had a bad, bad dream just now. I saw a crowd of people walking on top of a mountain. They were all dressed in white. Some of them were carrying a coffin."

"This is indeed a bad dream, Samuel, but what's it got to do with the prophet?"

"It was more than a dream. It was a message."

"A message from whom?"

"I guess, from God."

"How can you be sure?"

"I'm sure."

"Samuel, you're distressed because of the damn dream, but you'll forget it tomorrow and everything will be fine."

"It was more than a dream," Samuel repeated in a whisper. There was a deep sadness in his voice.

"You've just had a bad dream, that's all. Go back to sleep. We'll talk about it in the morning."

As much as he wanted to comfort Samuel, Danny was unable to stay awake.

But Samuel woke him up for the third time just before sunrise.

"What is it now, Samuel?"

"Your troubles are nearly over. The old man will accompany you and Abdelkadir to the main road the day after tomorrow. There'll be a military convoy arriving from Dolo. It'll take you to Neghelle."

"What do you mean?"

"You and Abdelkadir will be brought to Neghelle and from there Abdelkadir will be taken to his family."

"How do you know?"

"I know."

"And how about you?"

"I'll not be coming with you."

"What's wrong with you today?" This time Danny was very upset.

"Our ordeal is over. You've proved to be a tough boy. Life has prevailed. You'll grow up to become a great man one day. But you should remember this: no matter how vast and overwhelming the wilderness appeared to be, we were never lost. Farewell dear friend, I must now hurry to the funeral."

"Are you in earnest?"

"Yes, absolutely!"

"You'd leave me alone just because of a damn dream?"

"You'll be fine, of that much I'm sure. You'll be happy too and make many people happy."

Danny could not believe what he was hearing.

"You're becoming incomprehensible and irritating once again," he wept. Suddenly, he was filled with great anxiety.

"Don't be anxious, you'll be fine without me. Remember that some of your troubles are like that damn war. They are there and they're real, but you shall hear of them only from afar. They'll not destroy you. You'll prevail over them."

"Oh, Samuel, what are you saying?" fresh tears gushed from Danny's eyes. Instinctively, he sensed that something irreversible was about to happen.

"I'm going now. You can keep my jacket to remember me by. It was a gift from the prophet, I'm passing it on to you."

"Please, come to your senses!" Danny was so bewildered that he did not know what to do.

For a split second he thought he could be having a nightmare. So, he scrambled to get up.

"No, no, I'm not having a nightmare. This is real, awfully real," he mumbled to himself as he stood up.

But Samuel was already gone.

"Wait, Samuel, wait!" he shouted on top of his voice, rushing out of the hut. Samuel was nowhere to be seen.

"Oh, dear, I must be raving mad!" he said, great shock giving way to momentary but great relief. "Can it be that I was having a nightmare all along?"

The impact of what he had just experienced was so stunning that he had to support himself by leaning on the hut.

"What a nightmare!" he sighed.

He touched his cheeks, which were wet, and felt his anxiety resurfacing once again. He cautiously entered the hut and felt for Samuel with his hands in the dark. The place where Samuel had slept last night was empty. Indeed, there was no one in the hut except for Abdelkadir and himself.

"Samuel!" he shouted, at the top of his voice.

"What is it?" Abdelkadir moaned, raising himself to a sitting position.

"Samuel is gone!" Danny wailed.

"Where did he go?"

"I don't know. He's not here. Please, get up and help me. We must search for him."

Abdelkadir got up and they searched for Samuel everywhere they could think of, both inside and outside of the hut, but there was no trace of him.

"Why are you boys shouting?" The old man stepped out of the neighboring hut.

"Have you seen Samuel, the other boy?" Danny asked him, his eyes blurred with tears.

"He has left," the old man told him. "The soldier has also left. I will bring you two to the main road in two days' time. Rest for today, you don't have anything to do now."

"When did Samuel leave?"

"You mean the boy?"

"Yes."

"He left very early in the morning. My daughter-in-law saw him leaving. She said he was carrying a bag and a staff."

Danny rushed into the hut and searched for Samuel's jacket. It was there on the carpet, exactly where Samuel had left it. He slumped to his knees and wept unreservedly, clutching the jacket to his chest tightly, as if he would never let go.

"It's all right, son," the old man came to him and patted him on his shoulder. "Don't worry, I will bring you to the main road. A convoy will receive you. The soldier has settled everything. Don't weep."

But Danny was inconsolable. He wept until he had no strength left.

www.ingramcontent.com/pod-product-compliance
Lightning Source LLC
Chambersburg PA
CBHW020130310726
48970CB00006B/1801